A Tangled Book Web

Cynthia Gallant-Simpson

For Taylor who loves books, science, and her hometown.

Book loads of thanks to my bookshop guru advisor Jim Visbeck, owner of Isaiah Thomas Books, Cotuit, Cape Cod, Massachusetts without whom I could not have done this tale justice. Thanks Jim for your patience, kindness and amazing guidance as well as buckets of research and your decades-long experience as a book collector/seller. Loving books, libraries and bookstores does not make one an expert; that is why I needed Jim.

P.S. Jim has asked that I make it perfectly clear that he is not an expert on spiders. *

Thanks also from one painter to another. This book might never have been born were it not for a copy of Lois Taylor's wonderful painting of the beloved Cotuit pink bookstore that Jim sent to me that hangs over my desk. I admired it daily, promising myself that one of these days I would visit this intriguing looking shop and meet Jim in person. Then, one day the pink building began whispering. At first, almost imperceptibly until, over time, the voice became a shout.

The rest, as they say, is history.

My apologies to arachnologists for whatever errors I have made in dealing with spiders and their habits and talents. For the purposes of this book, I have taken liberties with these many-legged, talented, resourceful creatures.

September 24, 2016

Dear Professor Magus,

Speaking for the Harvard University Science Dept., your visit and talk scheduled for Tuesday November 17 will be the highlight of this year's investigation into the age old mystery of spider silk. The future of the mechanical properties of this amazing natural product, as you stated in your recent study conducted at your renowned laboratory promises numerous manufacturing and industrial applications.

I was particularly interested in your addendum: "The magic of spider silk has everything to do with the transmission of information through DNA. Human engineering, to date, has insufficient information as to how to do it better than Nature…thus beating Nature at its own game. Spider silk transforms from liquid protein to solid thread when it leaves the body. While scientists have been able to produce spider silk with the same biochemical integrity of the natural fibers for some time, it has remained beyond their abilities to re-create the mysterious *final spin* that results in aligning the fiber molecules, and increasing the fiber's tensile strength. That remaining mystery is what my laboratory experiments intend to solve."

A grand promise indeed!

Of particular interest is the high tensile strength of black widow silk, which, as you stated, is comparable in strength to Kevlar, carbon fiber and steel. Further, being lighter and of a lower density this would most certainly be of great interest for many commercial applications from bulletproof vests and aircraft bodies to bridge cables and medical sutures. Astonishing! We will speak further when you visit. Please let me know if there is anything additional you will need for your enlightening presentation.

Sincerely,

Arthur   Sedgewick   Ph.D.

ONE

"Please have a seat, Ms. Kavanagh. Coffee?"

"No thank you, don't do caffeine."

"Oh, terribly sorry. I have no caffeine-free hot drink to offer. I must correct that. Yes, I will address that oversight as soon as possible. Myself, I would probably be tucked up in a corner mewling by nine a.m. without my morning fix." He smiled and Libby slipped back in time. "Nasty stuff, caffeine. However, probably better than drugs…or should I say; *other drug*s?"

The attorney was so like his father, a man so revered by the town that his portrait hung prominently in the foyer of the Barnstable Court House where Libby had seen it years ago when her father brought her along to see where he worked. Libby gazed around the pleasant room on the second floor of the old Barnstable County Town Hall that had been renovated just a few years before for use as offices. Walking up the two flights of stairs rather than take the newly installed elevator, Libby had noted that there was another attorney's office, also a bookkeeper, and an ad agency. Three offices were still unoccupied. The name on the door, Attorney Benjamin West II, recalled that other elegant man of the same name who always wore grey suits to match his steel gray hair. She had met that man once, shortly before his death. She recalled that the father of the man sitting across the desk from her, apologizing for his caffeine habit, had practiced law back in the years when her father did.

This seemed like a dream, like time traveling back to a time and a place that she had packed away in her memory trunk. Like the sea captain's ledgers and other dusty memorabilia she loved to rummage through as a child, unlikely to be revisited soon.

Recalling the day the attorney's letter arrived at her narrow, tilted bookshop in Hastings, England Libby felt a shiver race down her spine. She clearly recalled how the astonishing news from Cape Cod had worked its way into and eventually altered her supposedly, perfectly ordered world with everything in its designated place, under her orderly control. Now, she wondered how she could ever again believe that she was the determiner of her own fate as she had for so long evidently fooled herself into believing. The thought hit her in her solar plexus, but was it a pain or something else?

Looking down, Libby smiled. The floors, handsome extra wide pine despite the ancient restrictions placed on early Cape Cod builders stating that boards over a certain width belonged to the king, glowed in the spring sunshine. The windows were nearly as tall as the walls, and the walls themselves had obviously been newly cleaned and refinished to look as if they had only been there for short years rather than more than a century. Libby, Elizabeth Hannah Kavanagh, was born just down the street in a house built by her great-great-grandfather, the sea captain Alfred Ebenezer Cobb who settled his family there near shops and the harbor where his ship returned, sometimes nearly a year after he departed for exotic places around the world. She knew the story of how he had finally retired, although still a young man, to build boats with his sons down at the harbor with a view of Sandy Neck across the narrow inlet. She wondered if it was still Howard Boats, run by a sweet man everyone called Bunny rather than his proper name, John Howard who bought the place from her family.

Up in the attic of the old family home, her mother's family, the Cobbs, Libby's spent rainy Saturdays, at least when she was not curled up in a comfortable chair in the front room of the library lost in books. Up among the cobwebs (believing that these gossamer spiders' webs were named for her family until someone corrected this) she pretended that she was the captain's daughter. Dressed as she loved to be in the old-fashioned dresses and hats packed away in the many steamer trunks, Libby was transported to an earlier time. Even as a young girl she could not fit her feet into the tiny leather boots once worn by Rebecca Elizabeth Cobb. Her mother told her that women's feet were far smaller back then. Libby had read about the practice of binding the feet of young

Chinese girls to prevent them from growing any larger. However, she did not ask if this was the reason. At least the dresses fit her perfectly. Once, she and her friend Katy put on as many of the petticoats they could each stuff under the dresses, laughing at how silly they looked in the full length mirror...*like overstuffed cream puffs*, as Katy said.

When Libby found the captain's ledgers, she lost herself in his adventures. Once, he sailed all the way to Tahiti, taking his wife and daughter along. The natives had seen white men before, but never white females. By then, the sailors who had mutinied against the nasty Captain Bligh had married the native women and forgotten those they left behind. Thus, the captain's wife and daughter were seen as exotic oddities and treated like goddesses who had arrived from heaven.

Now, sitting at the fine old oak desk whose neatness pleased her, looking much like her own, with everything in its proper place, Libby faced the man who had shaken up her world. No, she corrected herself; he had merely been the messenger. The man who had tossed and tumbled her world as if on a stormy sea was actually someone she had never met, let alone even knew existed.

Looking down at the papers neatly lined up on the handsome leather desk blotter (a lovely old-fashioned touch, Libby noted) the attorney read the instructions contained in the will.

"I, Grover Louis Cobb III, do hereby...."

Ending his reading, Attorney West looked up and smiled

Similar words Libby had read in the communication that eventually catapulted her from her cozy, satisfying life across the Atlantic, seeming like the theme of a new book she might consider ordering, had become real, not fiction. *I do hereby leave to my niece, daughter of my sister...my beloved bookshop...*

"I never heard of this man. If my mother had a brother, why didn't I know that, years ago? Even if they were estranged, wouldn't I have been told she had a brother?"

"In my experience, Eliz...Libby, families are sometimes strange and confusing to others. What I mean is..."

"What you mean is that my childhood included a big fat lie." Not meaning to sound bitter, because she was not, she had

3

seen enough of family feuds that affected generations, she smiled and shook her head.

"Well, I suppose your mother had her reasons. Everyone handles family grudges and disappointments differently. However, here is the proof. You may not have known of Grover Cobb's existence however he knew of yours. Even after you moved to England, he must have kept track of you."

"Oh. Why would you say that? I mean, although he knew about me because he kept up with my mother's life, what makes you think he actually kept track of me, Ben?"

"He added a note in the will that you could be found in Hastings at the By the Sea Bookshop. I guess no one can hide these days, Libby. I know that new age fact can have both good and bad results. However in this case, I do hope are pleased that it is so."

"Strange. Very, very strange. I wonder why he never communicated directly with me if he was suddenly so very concerned as an uncle...deciding to leave me his store is stranger than fiction. Yes, we had much in common...books, the business of books, but how could he have known that? Did no one else in town know? Why didn't someone tell me? Things like that never stay hidden in a small town like Barnstable. Although, come to think of it, I do recall my mother driving by a pink bookshop and my asking her why anyone would paint such a lovely old house pink." Ben said nothing, wanting her to continue her childhood reverie.

"Wait! I recall what she said about the place. She called it a 'sphere of bad influence', adding that the store sold books banned by decent people."

"Did she tell you the old stories about the Cobbs and the Winslows, Libby?" Ben got up to refill his coffee cup. Sitting back down, he remained quiet, watching Libby staring out the window as if she were not seeing the scenery but something no one else could see.

"Sure. As I recall, there was some ridiculous falling out years ago. Generations ago." She turned back to look at him. "I mean; something that happened way back in history, back when the two families first settled the town. I didn't pay much attention. However, what could it have been that would hang on for so damned long? Why would a family hold such a long grudge?"

4

Again, Libby seemed to leave the moment, finding something pressing beyond the window.

"It happens." Ben could easily imagine Libby in her own bookshop. He loved her British accent. Not fully developed, no, more like one still in the stages of arriving at officialdom. He wondered if everyone eventually picked up a local accent if they remained in a strange new place or if she had worked at it assiduously to guarantee that she fit in with the locals. When Libby remained quiet, as if she had checked out and her mind had drifted far away, Ben waited. Finally, he attempted to pull her back from wherever she was travelling in her mind.

"As I recall, there was an illegitimate child... At least, this is how my father told the story. A Cobb, a young man of twenty got a teenaged Winslow girl pregnant." Ben took a drink of the cooling coffee.

"Ah, that kind of old story. Interesting how families could turn against one another over such a thing and yet, we know it happened. An entire family blamed for one horny young man's behavior."

They both laughed. Libby removed her jacket and spread it on the back of her chair. The room had grown warm although the weather outside warned of a coming change. "Back then, as we know from history and literature, the Victorian female of the species was expected to remain virginal until marriage. It was the males who broke the rules. Of course, no one took into account the natural urges inherent in all animals, human and otherwise. However, what does that have to do with my mother and her brother?"

"I believe your uncle revived the old grudge. There was a Winslow girl; I believe her name was Abigail..."

Before Ben could finish, Libby asked, "Did we know each other growing up here, Ben?"

Ben laughed and leaned forward as if he were about to reveal a deep, dark secret.

"Well, actually, we did. I was a year behind you in school. I was that funny looking kid with the buck teeth and hair that refused to be tamed. Once, you called me a weirdo."

"Oh damn. Oh, I am so very sorry. Damn it, kids can be so cruel."

5

"No problem, I grew into my teeth and my mother's hair dresser gave me a makeover. Taught me to use conditioner and come in for a trim once a month."

"Oh, no. That was you? I am so ashamed. I recall now that I called you Bengie the Bug! Oh, sorry... so very sorry; I did it on a dare. I could just die right here where I sit. Quick, I need to dictate my will!" *So, Bengie the Bug grew into a very good looking man. Wonder if he is single.* Then, she realized that she hadn't wondered that about any man since Quentin Avery walked out her life.

TWO

"Shall we begin fresh, Libby?"

"Oh, yes, please, let's do. Promise I will never again call you Bengie the Bug. "

"Thank you. I trust you, therefore I will not insist upon getting that in writing."

"Let me simply say this however, before we continue. The kids used to call me Bookworm. They expected me to object however I was quite delighted." Libby hopes this might go a bit of a way toward making amends for childhood misbehavior.

"So, you were a worm and I a bug. But we showed them, didn't we?"

Libby smiled, folded her hands on the desk and sat at attention. "Phew, glad that is all out of the way so we can move on to more important things, Benjamin. May I call you Benjamin or do you prefer Sir?" Her grin brought one from him and the room suddenly felt warmer and less formal.

"Ben, please. Here is what I know about your uncle and mother and their...shall we say, disagreement. Nowadays-I am happy to announce, the Cobbs and the Winslows have forgotten the old rift that made enemies of their families for generations. Water under the bridge, as they say. Well, correction: Winifred Winslow, who, at nearly one-hundred years of age is as spry as a chicken, will gladly relate the story about the Pitcairn Island misunderstanding to anyone willing to listen. The kids call her The Wicked Witch of Barnstable and I do believe that she is proud of the moniker."

Libby smiled and nodded her head. "I remember her well. She once called the dog warden demanding that he shoot my dear, sweet beagle, Jennifer, claiming that the dog ate her tulips and must be shot at once. Fortunately, Sam Williams was not just the dog warden; he also raised beagles and was a strong proponent of the breed as a perfect pet for children as they were a sweet and trustworthy breed. Jennifer came from his brood. He knew she was an angel who never misbehaved."

Ben smiled and slowly shook his head, recalling his own run-ins with the "witch."

Libby sat back in the chair, anxious to get on with the meeting that promised to finally explain a lot of things about her family. "Before we got off on another track, you began a tale about my uncle and another Winslow girl, not so much ancient history as the old family grudge. I can only assume that my secret uncle repeated the evil deed with yet another sweet innocent female from the hated Winslow family. Naughty, naughty; what is the family coming to? Did he marry her?"

Before Ben could answer, once again Libby was drawn to the sky slowing becoming laced with loose, frilly white clouds that she knew were the prelude to the rain soon to follow. Nimbus clouds. Latin for rain.

"No, he did not marry the girl. Her name was Rebecca Marie Winslow. It seems that Grover was not the marrying kind. Kind of a mixed bag kind of guy, you might say. A Born Again Christian, he was, according to my grandfather, furious that she insisted upon telling everyone that he was the father. Naturally, he denied the fact vociferously, calling Rebecca a liar and a tart. Everyone who believed Rebecca and knew his ways understood that in Grover's mind the child was living proof of his sin. It seems that he believed that he could fool around as long as no living proof transpired. He earnestly believed that God would not condemn him for his misdeed without solid evidence of said misdeed.

"Certainly was a weird man. I now see why my mother chopped off the limb on the family tree where that nut was hanging."

"I like your sense of humor, Libby. Just to complete the picture for you, Grover refused to acknowledge the boy's parentage and although Rebecca begged him to allow her to bring Seth to the shop, sure that he would see how similar they were, he refused this, as well. Once, when Seth was ten years old, when his mother brought him back to town to visit family, Seth attempted to visit his father at the bookshop. When he told Grover that he was his son, the man tossed books at the boy and chased him down the street shouting, Devil's spawn!"

"Gotta love the irony, Ben."

"Well, his mother named him Seth Jeremiah Winslow after the family sea captain who went head to head with your Captain Cobb in that other family feud. Something about treasure on Pitcairn Island that the two captains fought over. Unfortunately, in the way of young boys, and I suppose because Seth was much like his nasty father, the other boys taunted him, calling him Corn Cobb."

"Yes, my mother told me about a number of old family feuds between the Cobbs and the Winslows. Seems that Winslow got the gold mine and Cobb got the shaft as the old country song goes. So, not only did I have a secret uncle but also a secret cousin? Seth would be about ten years old than me. It seems inconceivable in such a small community that I never heard that we were cousins. I always wanted cousins. I am beginning to feel as if my childhood was a complete hoax."

"As I recall, Seth's mother took him to live in Falmouth or Bourne where she became a school teacher. Evidently, Seth was a brilliant student despite his unfortunate personality. Science. Qualified for early entrance into MIT but his mother did not have the money for tuition so she sent him to ask his father whose bookstore was very successful at the time. Not selling porn as your mother implied, but specializing in Cape Cod books, rare and collectibles, but also contemporary local writers whose subject matter was the Cape. You know, Thoreau and such. Well, the old man did not care a damn about Seth's education and sent him packing. You see, your Uncle Grover, hated science. He was a devout Christian who believed that God decided everything and that all scientists were dangerous charlatans interfering with the natural order of things. Thus, when his only child decided to become one of them evil, *interferin' sinners*, naturally Grover refused to pay his tuition. Wonder if things might have been different if the prodigal son had been another Thoreau."

"So, who paid the brilliant boy's tuition?"

"MIT stepped up with scholarships. Also, someone in town pitched in when the story got around about his mean father. No one knows who, however."

Libby grew quiet. The sky darkened and the first raindrops fell. When she turned back to Ben, he continued. He was growing used to these interruptions that he assumed were Libby's need to time travel back to her childhood in Barnstable. He felt both guilty for forcing this reverie upon her if she had chosen to forget when she moved to England and hopeful that it would be helpful in convincing her to remain there. He could easily imagine her running the pink bookshop, charming customers with her British accent and her lovely demeanor, not to mention her obvious broad knowledge and innate talent for the book business. So far, Elizabeth Cobb Kavanagh was charming him with her quick, if subtle sense of humor in addition to being lovely to look at. Funny, he thought, how an unknown to her curmudgeon uncle's genes had been passed onto this lovely, bright, charming woman. Fortunately for her, not also his weird personality. He liked that she was obviously a consummate professional. Then, when he least expected it, she would slip in some comment that broke him up. Ah, woman!

"Interesting tale, Libby, about the day Seth came to beg for the money. As the story goes, father and son argued volubly in the shop and then out onto the street. Neighbors came out of their houses and shops and eventually the police arrived to break up the argument that had by then become a fist fight. When the cops tried to restrain Grover he broke way and ran down the street screaming that Seth was a *living sin, an aberration on God's earth*. Or words to that affect."

"I assume that Seth is no longer with us or my erstwhile uncle would have left him Cobb Hill Books. Should I be grateful that I am an also ran? Or, just a dumb luck heir?"

"Ah, therein, my dear lady lies the rub, as our friend Shakespeare would say. No, Seth is alive and well and runs a prestigious lab in South Boston. Yes, Professor Seth Magus is an arachnologist; I believe that is the correct term. Specializes in spiders."

"Spiders, hm. Curiouser and curiouser by the moment. Wait, Seth Magus, not Cobb?"

"Yes, he legally changed his name, evidently not wishing to carry on either the Winslow or the Cobb family names."

"Ah, as I recall, a magus is a member of a hereditary priestly class among the ancient Medes and Persians. Upstart, that cousin of mine! Oh, I should have stayed where I was safe and content in lovely Hastings by the Sea. Am I having a nightmare? Did I make a mistake and take a hallucinatory drug rather than an aspirin? Ah, perhaps this is simply an aberration brought on by jet lag."

Ben laughed although fearful that Libby might be seriously considering returning to England with a bundle of cash from the sale of the troublesome inheritance that had come her way. Suddenly, he wanted to cross his fingers, find a four leaf clover, or perhaps simply beg her to remain and take over the successful book business that had brought her to his office.

"As you probably remember, the building that now houses the pink bookshop is a lovely old place. Built in the early nineteenth century by another sea captain, back in the days when seemingly every third man on the Cape and Islands owned his own ship. Back then, a successful sea captain could afford to establish his family in a lovely, large and gracious home before heading back to sea, sometimes for years at a time. Lucky for us we get to enjoy these lovely historic homes, particularly along the Old King's Highway.

"Oh, I do wish people would return to that moniker. Despite there being no more king in the mix, therefore, politically incorrect, it was such a fine old name for Main Street. How I detest hearing the long road from the bridge over the canal all the way down the peninsula to Provincetown referred to as route 6A. Ugh!" Ben nodded in agreement.

"So true. I prefer Main Street. Always use that rather than the route number that sounds so un-Cape like. Just for a moment, let me say that it was those long trips undertaken by our ancestor sea captains that made for such strong, independent women who did things such as establishing libraries, start and run local businesses, and hold positions on town boards for which there were no interested or qualified males."

"Yes, notable, indeed. I once read a book about Nantucket where the women were also left behind when the men were, as the history books put it, *off on the whale*. Had it not been for them the island would have fallen into disarray. Interesting lesson there for

11

the men of today; the knob heads who underestimate the power of women."

"You do not have to sell me, Libby. I have all the respect in the world for the great women of this world. Here is a bit of history that will interest you, Libby. The bookshop was once the home of the only doctor on the upper-Cape. Because there was no hospital any closer than Boston, the man kept a few rooms for seriously ill patients and he did some surgery. The other choice was a long, bumpy trip by horse wagon over rutted dirt roads to Boston. Most preferred to remain here and die rather than be jostled and probably die anyway from the arduous trip."

"Then it became a book store." Libby pulled her jacket from the back of the chair and put it over her shoulders.

"Are you cold? I can turn up the heat if you like."

"Oh, no, thanks. I just have this way of feeling the weather in my bones. Some kind of weird barometer built in to the body. Go on, please, more history lesson, please."

"Well, Grover Cobb bought the building years later, but in the meantime it was a bakery, an inn, and a ladies' clothing store. It was Grover's mistress who decided to paint the building pink with green shutters. Grover hated it, but loved her, so, even after she died it remained pink, newly painted every ten to fifteen years in her honor."

"Ah, at least the old codger knew it was best not to interfere with a strong woman. But pink…so not traditional Cape Cod."

Ben laughed, enjoying himself far more than he had ever expected from just a regular day, as his mother kiddingly referred to his work, *Doing law stuff.*

"Now, here is the other part of your uncle's will."

"No, spare me, please. He left me his collection of stuffed ostriches, as well?"

"No, sorry to disappoint. He left his home in Osterville to Seth. So little was known about the man who owned the bookshop, no one knew that although he lived over the shop he also owned this house on the water that he never occupied. Unfortunately a fire in the town hall years ago destroyed all the old records so I cannot tell you when he bought it although Winifred the Witch claims that he won it in a poker game. However, because he believed the house was cursed he never occupied it. The curiosity is that he never sold it. It was once a fine place before he left it abandoned to become rather dilapidate. Needs paint and repairs as well as someone to remove years of fallen trees and vines that have invaded to make it look like something out of a horror movie. Either he forgave his son for being born or in the end he decided that family matters despite having disappointed him."

Again, Libby slipped away and Ben sat silent, waiting for her to return. Now, the rain was coming down in a torrent, transporting her back home to England. Over time, having lived for a short time in London where the dreary weather downed her spirits, once she owned the bookshop she grew far more fond of the wet days, days when people took refuge in the shop and often left with book purchases. She wondered if the very capable friend she left in charge was managing to make the many pots of tea and put out the daily bakery delivery of half-size sconces the baker made especially for her every morning. This rain outside the window drew her to it, causing her a sense of unease. What on earth was she to do with another bookshop, one on the other side of the Atlantic?

Returning, she looked at Ben and smiled. "Sorry, daydreaming. Terribly impolite. So, cannot wait to meet my cousin. I honestly do not know at this time what I will do about the bookshop, Ben, but I do appreciate all the family history, sordid as it happens to be. Spiders, eh? What kind of man chooses spiders as his life's purpose, I wonder?"

The icy shiver that flashed down her spine took Libby by surprise. Yes, the room had grown cooler as the weather changed but she refused to be a complaining, fragile woman insisting upon wasting fuel just to warm her bones. Just a bit of leftover jet lag, she told herself. She did need a nap, for sure. Slipping into her navy blue linen jacket, she suddenly could not wait to return to the room at the inn for a good long nap before dinner at the Dolphin. Noticing that the restaurant was still there in its prominent location on Main Street, Libby had promised herself that she would go there that evening for their superb clam chowder. Real, New England chowder, so thick a spoon could almost stand up in it, not thin chowder like everywhere else. Yum.

Only months later would Libby recall that shot of ice down her spine that, at the time, she considered to be nothing more than a bit of leftover jet lag. Oh, if only everything that transpired after she took ownership of the Cobb's Hill Bookshop had turned out to be as simple and understandable as the need for a good nap. She was adept at dealing with things that challenged the rational intellect. Some said her bookshop was haunted by a man murdered during the WWI who was deemed a spy and taken down by a group of townspeople, then secretly buried under the floorboards. Sometimes, just as she was closing up for the day, she heard a kind of low wail coming from under the service desk. Just a creaking board, as she preferred to believe, unwilling to admit that it sounded very much like someone in pain. However, as she did with all challenges, both in the business realm and the ghostly realm; she applied patient intellectual perseverance and rational consideration.

Then, she recalled the words of one of her most favorite brainiacs: *I never made one of my discoveries through the process of rational thinking.* Albert Einstein

THREE

"Good morning, welcome to the Cape Cod Standard Times advertising pages. How may I help you?"

"Hello. Lovely day. I could get used to no morning fog. I would like to place an ad in the help wanted section of your newspaper, please."

"Of course. Would you like to fill this out or, if you prefer, you can dictate your ad and I will create it for you."

"I have it here. This is what I wish to advertise however not until next week. Shall we say, Wednesday? Or, better yet, perhaps you might advise me as to which day is most likely to attract someone looking for work."

"Well, hm, interesting. So you are the new owner of the bookstore. I knew the former owner. Not a very nice man. Oh, sorry, was he a friend? There I go putting foot in said mouth, once again."

"No problem. My name is Elizabeth Cobb Kavanagh, and yes the former, now deceased owner was my uncle. I hope to be running the store as soon as the legalities are dealt with." Listening to herself she realized that she sounded like an American again. If she were still in England she'd have spoken with far more discretion. She had quickly learned when she moved there that the British never share any more personal information than is absolutely necessary. If possible, one should even speak in riddles to avoid having others know one's business.

"Oh, I am soooo sorry. Please forgive me. My condolences. I did not mean to…well, I am sure he must have been a good person if a bit grumpy, now and then. Probably had his reasons. After all, you cannot love books and be all bad."

15

Libby smiled, wondering how many times she would have to face this kind of reaction to her deceased uncle's lasting impression on the village. Hopefully, once she reopened the bookshop, out of curiosity people would stop by to check her out, and then she could gradually erase nasty Grover Cobb's stain. From what Ben said, most of the business that kept the shop going came from tourists interested in Cape Cod books. Fortunately, Grover had specialized in books written about the Cape and/or by Cape authors. This gave him an edge on the book market in a place where every town had more than one bookshop. The majority of the inventory was rare and collectibles however, he also stocked some more recent work by living Cape Cod authors and others who, if not long gone, had made their indelible mark on the peninsula.

"Please, no apologies required. He was a miserable codger, first cousin to a rattlesnake and no one liked him, not even his family. I inherited the shop and things will change when I take over. There will be hot tea and crumpets or whatever is most appealing to local tastes always available. There will be sitting areas where customers can read undisturbed with no pressure to buy a book. More of a library setting than a commercial bookshop. So, what day would be best for my ad?"

"What a relief. Sounds lovely. I love books, but after the first few times I simply had to give up and drive down to either Brewster or Dennis or even as far as Orleans where there are very friendly bookstores. I would rather remain on Main Street you see, rather than go into Hyannis. Do you know the area? I mean, did you already know the Cape when you inherited? Oops, so sorry. None of my business. I was very impolite. What day would you like the ad run, Miss?"

Libby smiled and reassured the pretty young woman that she was neither insulted nor upset by her personal questions. Actually, she thought, this is quite refreshing. Very American. After all, if she was going to take over her uncle's business she would do best to do as the locals do.

"Very kind of you, Miss. I tend to be nosy. Not with any ill intent, but simply because I love people. I am a writer when I am not earning a living here. As someone who is in the book business I hope you understand that the best writers are those who study human nature. Oops, there I am going off again. So, I believe that Saturday is the day people check the help wanted ads. Are you by any chance from England? I love your accent. And, by the way, if you served crumpets I think it would be so delightful. Of course, no one around here in any of the bakeries makes them, so maybe…"

"I'm sorry, I did not catch your name, Miss."

"Katy. Katy Dobbs."

"You have been so helpful Ms. Dobbs and yes, I have been living in England for many years. However, I was born right here. Right in the village in fact. I am also a Cobb. Well, my mother was. The old curmudgeon who left me his bookshop was my uncle, Grover Cobb, my mother's brother."

"Oh, sure. I know a lot about the Cobb family. I love local history. When will you be opening the shop? I cannot wait to have a friendly place like you describe right here in the village. My mother has a bakery and you might ask her about making crumpets. Oh, sorry, probably not supposed to do that. However, she is a wonderful baker and I am sure she would love to make authentic British crumpets."

"Katy, I have loved our visit, we must do it again some time. I will stop in to speak with your mother at her bakery."

"Great. It's behind the general store. Used to be a thrift shop but it closed. It is called, Sweets by the Sea. Mom's name is Carrie."

You have been most helpful on a number of concerns I have had. When I have the tea table set up I will call and let you know that is it time to visit."

Help Wanted

Enthusiastic cleaner/organizer to work with new owner of a bookstore. Respect for books a must. If you have a distaste for or an allergy to dust, dirt, bugs or mold you need not apply. Apply in person Cobb's Hill Bookshop, Main Street, Barnstable Village.

FOUR

The Barnstable Court House was bustling when Libby entered the foyer feeling nervous as a cat napping under a rocking chair as her grandmother used to say. She told herself not to be silly. Stopping to look at some lovely old portraits of prominent townspeople in the front hall, she smelled coffee. Not tea, but coffee. Turning she found a gray-haired women standing close by holding a paper cup marked Dunkin' Donuts. The aroma wafting from that cup melted her heart, sending her back, back in time.

Her mother was standing at the kitchen stove, her father sitting at the wonderful old pine kitchen table where, as her mother pointed out to her when she was very young, *these grooves were worn into the table by centuries of women kneading bread, dear.* Often, Libby would run her fingers over the gentle but clearly visible marks on the tabletop, sure she could smell yeast. Every morning, when she entered the kitchen, she smelled it, the warm and inviting aroma of freshly made coffee. That and the other kitchen fragrances that could still awaken sense memories of home. She read once, in her psych class in college, that smell memories are the strongest and longest lasting. Her mother's gingerbread or apple crisp baking, sent out what, in Libby's mind's eye, seemed like loving invitations to that wonderful kitchen of her childhood. Like arms beckoning, promising love and security. Nothing like either of those warm and delectable desserts to make right a difficult school day or a disagreement with a friend. Even after her parents died and she moved permanently to England, she regularly cooked both ginger bread and apple crisp, thinking she did this simply because they were her favorite desserts. Now, she realized that doing so was for a deeper, more profound reason. Home. That earliest homeplace.

Heading for the stairs, Libby thought about what lay ahead. She had done it. She had left Hastings, left England and returned home to Barnstable, to the Cape Cod that formed her, the place she had been so sure would never draw her back again. Never say never!

She told herself that when she once again stepped out into the lovely day that was so very different from Hastings at this time of year, she would begin the first steps in a most unexpected professional life altering experience. One that, quite surprisingly, came with a chance to return home thrown in for good measure…that's why they call such things surprises. Home. How strange that sounded; like finding one's self catapulted back in time to a place and time belonging to someone else entirely. Had she really become someone else? Surely, she had worked at trying to make that happen. She had done it for love only to find that love can have a sell by date just like stale bread.

Well, as she had been telling herself daily since making her decision to re-do her life that she thought was indelibly cast and solidly baked in British clay, it was also time to rewrite those life guidelines she was so stubbornly sure she would never, ever, alter. Soon, she would enter the courtroom to sit by her attorney and new friend Ben West II a dedicated and proud Cape Codder. Oh, how she liked Ben. She had not told him however, she credited him, not her uncle, with guiding her ship of life into a better port, setting her off on a completely unexpected tack. Full sail ahead! She knew better than to tell him how it seemed that Fate had brought her to his office in particular for reasons far more potent than that her Uncle Grover's death had set the ball rolling. No, she would never tell Ben how she was beginning to feel about him. She had learned her lesson only too well than to expect love to last. There, she said the word, LOVE. She had scrubbed that weakness from her soul with harsh lye soap. No more love of that kind for Libby Cobb Kavanagh. No thanks. Better by far that she get herself a trusted and loving dog. No, maybe it was time for another cat. A bookshop cat like in so many novels. She would call him Shakespeare but if a girl, then, Ophelia. Yes, great idea.

The air around her crackled with the voices of lawyers and their clients, people seeking dog licenses and fishing licenses, a small child crying about a fallen candy bar swooped up in a tissue by her parent and a bunch of teenagers being led by a woman who seemed to be their teacher who kept shushing them and motioning for them to bunch up and not take up so much room. *Damn! This is the first day of the rest of my life. Holy shit, I cannot believe this is not a dream.*

Recalling the day she left for England to spend a year studying at London University, the opportunity of a lifetime, her dream come true, she climbed to the second floor where she would be legally pronounced the owner of her new bookshop, Libby smiled. As a young woman she viewed the immediate future to be a magical country where she would study Shakespeare in the place where he walked and wrote and fell in love. She would call upon the spirit of Virginia Wolfe and finally get the chance to castigate her for shoving all those heavy rocks into her coat pocket and then drowning herself, in her so talented prime. Her list of things to do was long. She meant to stand on the time line at the Greenwich Observatory. To eat fish and chips in the place where they were born...with a liberal does of malt vinegar. To walk across all the bridges spanning the Thames, and so much more. Each and every thing on her list she accomplished. Not there was falling in love and yet she entered into that British experience fully and trustingly. Ah, youth is wasted on the young, indeed. A year later, while still students, she and Reginald, "Reggie" Thornstrum married, and thus began her disillusionment. Well, no time for such thoughts now, Libby told herself as she entered the courtroom. There he was, Attorney Benjamin West II looking dapper and charming. Stick to business Libby, she told herself as she slipped in to sit beside her new friend.

Leaning over, Libby whispered in Ben's ear. "Did I tell you that my Hastings shop was no wider than a stingy wedge of cake and was inserted between the two adjoining buildings so badly constructed that the one on the left leaned in and the one on the right leaned out and in between my bookshop tilted like a ship with a busted rudder?"

Ben turned to look at her and smiled. "Congrats, this is the first day of the rest of your life, Libby."

"So, Sir, is my erstwhile cousin in attendance? Cannot wait to see him; never been close up to a mighty magus."

Ben leaned closer to Libby. Up close, her scent was even nicer. He thought it was bayberry but he had never known that anyone bottled the quintessential Cape Cod scent.

20

"No, he refused the invitation. His attorney will represent him today. Word around town is that he will have the old house torn down and build a new one. Thankfully, the zoning laws will not permit a super-modern house there because of the historic zoning restrictions. The Historic Commission is peopled with fanatic worshippers of historical architecture so we have no worries there. Heard they pack guns for those fools who try to fight them to build space age houses. Just kidding about the guns however, they can be quite formidable when challenged." Ben wanted to touch her, take her hand perhaps, but he knew better. They were still only professional associates but he hoped...

Fourteen minutes later it was done. Libby was the new owner of the Cobb's Hill Bookshop with full legal rights to continue the business there despite the more recent zoning in the area that excluded any new commercial operations. Pre-existing laws protected the oddly painted pink shop under new ownership. Sitting there warmed by the sunlight coming in the tall windows Libby recalled the phrase, *grinning like an ape.* She hoped she was not doing so on the outside however, she most definitely was on the inside. She had to admit that she had had serious reservations about leaving England, leaving the charming seaside village of Hastings, her tightly packed, oddly leaning, forever musty and damp little bookshop and her wonderful friends of twenty-odd years. Now, however, nothing had felt so very right in a long time. Or so Libby told herself. The other Libby, the one who thought she had full control and would forevermore, the Libby who only drank tea made in an old silver teapot with a built-in strainer, poured into lovely white porcelain cups embellished with pink roses, had vanished and been replaced by the Libby who stopped at the nearest Dunkin'Donuts for her daily espresso in a paper cup. Soon, she promised herself, she would unpack the new fancy coffee brewer she ordered on Amazon and the ten navy blue mugs with a white stripe running around the mid-section emblazoned with the words, Cobb's Hill Books.

Libby waited for Ben to replace his papers into his briefcase. She looked around the room and wondered how many of the people there today would leave the courthouse feeling as excited and filled with eager anticipation as she felt at that moment. Probably damned few of them! Divorces, property disputes, legal actions that inevitable leave one or both of the parties unhappy and in some cases devastated must, she told herself, invest courtrooms with heavy emotions that, akin to ghosts, remain forever trapped within the walls.

The word gratitude leapt into her mind as Ben spoke to another lawyer and then to a woman Libby had watched appear before the judge looking defeated only to perk up and seem to glow when he moved in her favor. Not Ben's client, however they obviously knew one another because she hugged him tightly, happy tears in her eyes.

Gratitude is an interesting thing, Libby told herself. For instance, at that moment she overflowed with gratitude to an uncle she had never met, never knew existed, and yet he had left her his business. Then, realizing that for some crazy reason the thought had not entered her consciousness, it hit her that Uncle Grover might have left her a grocery store, a barbershop, or a boat shop instead of a bookstore. Just weird luck or some universal righting of family wrongs? Did he somehow know that she owned one in England? Had he traced her whereabouts as anyone could do so easily since good old Google came onto the scene, and knew that she would probably treasure his beloved shop? At least, she liked the idea that he left her the bookshop rather than the house. It had to mean that he wanted her to have what he had loved for so many years. Her mother had been so old school. So protective of appearances, of standing in the community, of the importance of old Barnstable family names…a Charlotte Bronte leftover. Things no modern person cared a fig about. However, she tried to understand that being a born and bred a Cape Codder, a citizen of Barnstable, the prominent town and the county, even if only a few decades ago, her mother had grown up in a very different time.

Charlene Cobb had been unable to forgive her only sibling for crossing the invisible, so artificial and out of date social line between the two prominent families, the Cobbs and the Winslows. She wondered if they had been close as children, she and her brother. Grover Cobb has transgressed all that was mighty and important to this ancient family of snobs. Fortunately, her mother had not imbued her with this silly out of date and definitely not mourned attitude.

Ben motioned to Libby who, once again he noticed, was obviously daydreaming. Funny how this kind of habit of wandering away in the middle of a serious legal meeting in his office or in court when the client ought to be fully present would have annoyed him if it had been anyone but Libby. She did look changed, happy and more rested than she had since that first day in his office. Since then, she had thrown herself into making plans for up-dating the owner residence over the shop, surprising him that she intended to live there. At that moment, he wanted to touch her, maybe just to take her arm and pull her up from the bench. Everything was finally legally settled and she had decided to remain in town to run the bookshop. He could not be happier.

"Time to go, new owner of the Cobb's Hill Bookshop."

"Funny isn't it that Cobb's Hill was once referred to as a mountain?"

Ben laughed. "Obviously you have been boning up on local history. Hey, you ought to…well, once you are settled and the business is rolling along nicely, you ought to join the Historic Commission. You would be a fine addition."

Following Libby out of the courtroom, Ben wondered if he should ask her to lunch. Out in the hall a pretty young woman sat crying in the arms of an older man. Two children were sitting on the floor gazing intently at a creepy looking spider. Libby wanted to caution them about touching it recalling that despite her former belief that there were no deadly spiders on the Cape, she had found out different. Should she perhaps speak to the woman who appeared to be their mother who sat grinning into space unaware of her children? No. Instead, she simply headed for the door, anxious to breathe in fresh salt air. To fill her lungs with the wonderful fresh Cape air that she had grown up with, special beyond any air she had ever inhaled.

Stepping out onto the granite steps, Libby stopped and looked up at the sunny sky. Not a cloud in sight. Another perfect day with no rain on the horizon. She had so loved Hastings, her little flat above the tiny, tilted bookshop, the precious women friends she made when she joined the local Women's Institute and learned to knit and yet, there was entirely too much rain there.

"This granite beneath your feet, Libby Cobb came from Maine."

23

"Sorry, did you say something, Ben?"

"I said that these granite steps," he pointed to their feet, "came from a quarry in Maine as was all the other granite used in the building of this handsome courthouse. You have probably climbed the one hundred and sixteen steps of the Pilgrim Monument in Provincetown but did you know that it too was built with Maine granite?"

Libby laughed. It felt so good laughing out in the fresh air where she could just manage to catch the floating scent of bayberry. "I did not know that. Did you know that I found someone who wants to buy my shop in Hastings?"

"Really. Terrific. That did not take long. Someone you know or a stranger looking for an escape from London to the country, to the lovely coast?"

"Have you ever been to Hastings, Ben?"

"As a matter of fact, I have. Yes, my parents took my brother and me there when we spent a few weeks in England when I was young. I still have a t-shirt emblazoned with a crumbling castle, the British flag, and in large numbers the date ten-sixty-six."

"Oh, so when I speak about the town you can see it in your mind's eye. Oh, lovely. Well, yes, a friend of a friend who visited often, and for whom I located some lovely rare editions, has put a down-payment on the shop. I will be removing some of the contents, of course. Things that I treasure and will have no trouble finding a market for here."

"Oh, so you will be going back to pack up, of course. Silly I hadn't thought about that."

"Yes, in ten days I will take a flight from Boston and be gone for a week only. I don't actually have much to retrieve beyond those books I mentioned. I lived rather sparsely in my little tight space above the shop. The flat, er, sorry, still on Brit speak. I mean the apartment above the new shop will seem truly luxurious. Right now it is a nasty mess. My uncle certainly had no interest in making a cozy home there. However, once cleaned, newly painted and as soon as I find some furniture it should be quite cozy for me and Shakespeare."

"So, you have a nice collection of William's works then?"

"What? Oh, yes, the William Shakespeare. Yes, however in this case I speak of my dear newly adopted calico cat. He seems to like the name."

"You certainly do not waste any time, Libby Kavanagh. Is he staying with you at the inn?" Ben's question was filled with the sound of confusion. What innkeeper, he wondered would go along with such a transaction?

"I know. What a lovely surprise when Mary Ellen said that it would be fine until my flat...uh, apartment over the shop is ready. She loves cats so she let me set up a litter box for him in a large wooden box she had in the cellar. He is so well behaved and seems to love me as much as I love him."

"Of course he does." Not for the first time, Ben wondered about Libby's love life. She must have had one being so lovely and sweet and lovable, he reasoned. Yet, she never mentioned leaving a man behind in England....or one who would be arriving soon to join her there. He hoped there was no one. When she was ready he wanted to be the one she chose. Cautioning himself that he had to be very, very patient, he just smiled. He had to allow her to settle in. She had so many changes to make, so many things to become re-accustomed to that would certainly take months. Anyway, he too loved cats, so that was a good start.

Driving out of the court parking area Ben stopped before pulling onto Main Street. "How about a celebratory lunch at the Dolphin, Libby?"

"Oh, that would be lovely. Amazing that they are still in business. So many restaurants have a short life span these days. I would love to join you. We have much to celebrate."

Ben drove across the street into the parking lot for the Barnstable Market. Continuing on, he turned right to access the parking lot for all of the stores in that block. They entered through the rear entrance to the restaurant and headed for a table for two by the closed off fireplace.

"Ben, how's the law business? Might need to talk to you about something...later, of course."

"Libby, this is Marge Crocker, she and her husband own the place."

"So nice to meet you Marge... Wait, the Margery Crocker goalie who won every field hockey game for our team because she was, as they said in the Standard Times, *"faster than lightening on her feet and twice as fiery"*?

"You two were in school together?"

"Yup, we were." Hugging Libby, Marge said, and you Bookworm, were a lousy player!"

"I confess. My father insisted that I take up at least one sport to make friends. He was sure if I did not stop spending so much time reading I would end up... Well, I guess he was somewhat correct, I ended up tied to books in many ways."

"Oh, yes, you inherited the crazy Grover's shop! Sorry, but you must know that the man was a weirdo. So, you two were related. Never made the connection."

Later, after a delicious lunch and lots of catching up from Ben on town changes since she'd been gone, Libby announced that she had to get back to the inn to feed Shakespeare. "He doesn't like breakfast. Instead, he prefers to eat in the early afternoon. Lucky for him I will always be there to cater to his preferences and needs. Being a bookshop cat seems to fit the bill for the little guy. Not that he knows it yet but he will be perfect for the position."

"Lucky kitty." Ben wondered if Shakespeare could teach him to purr.

FIVE

"Good morning, Miss Kavanagh. Thanks so very much for considering me for the job. I would just love working here with you in this great store. My mother brought me here when I was very young and I bought a book with money my grandmother gave me for my birthday. It had old pictures of the Cape and lots of interesting history."

"Katy, I am so pleased that you answered my ad. However, I hope you are not making a wrong move. With your people skills you might do better at the newspaper. I mean, if you had planned to move along and perhaps become a news writer."

"Oh, no, it was always a temp thing. I prefer old news to new news." Katy laughed and Libby fully understood her meaning.

"So do I. Well, if you are willing to begin your new career as a simple cleaning woman…alongside me, of course, then you are hired. Later, I will teach you the business, from the ground up as they say. Right now, if we do not clean up this place we might get closed down by the Board of Health before we get a chance to do the other, more interesting things."

Katy laughed. "My father is on the Board of Health so have no fears. Anyway, when we get this place cleaned you will probably be awarded the best town business site improvement medal, Ms. Kavanagh."

"Well, I feel far safer. Now, first thing is that you must call me Libby. We are two ambitious, independent women taking on something that a man messed up."

"Well, Libby, I for one know that anything a man can do so can I. My mother has always reminded me of that. Oh, you must meet her, she's great."

"I did meet her just the other day. We discussed scones and other British baked goods. She reads British crime novels, as she told me. She is going to make lovely sweets for the tea table just as soon as we are ready."

"Terrific. So what do you want me to do first?"

"I didn't expect you to start today, Katy. When do you leave the paper job?"

"Already did. I know. You are going to say what Mom did. What if you don't hire me and I have already quit the paper. I knew the job was mine the minute I placed your ad for you."

Libby laughed. "You are a most remarkable young woman, Katy. We are going to make a terrific pair. Well, let me see. Let us begin with dragging lots of dusty boxes out of under the counters, from the closets and from every place my uncle managed to push them so we can decide what to save and what to jettison. I do believe he was a world-class hoarder. As we move along I will educate you as to what must be done when handling old books. They damage quite easily and even the slightest damage can destroy their value to a serious collector."

Six long and dusty hours later, Libby and Katy come up for air suddenly realizing how hungry they are.

"Hello. Anyone want a freshly baked croissant drowning in gruyere cheese and ham?"

"Mom. Wow. Starving.

"Oh, Carrie, you are sent from heaven. I am so sorry to have kept Katy so busy we almost forgot to eat…that is, until both of our stomachs groaned in unison. Oh, they smell lovely."

Sitting outside on the narrow front porch on a bench that Libby made a mental note to replace as it was about to collapse, she closed her eyes and lifted her dust covered face to the sun. "You know, I do miss England, Hastings and my funny tilted bookshop however, I had forgotten, I now realize; how much I need the sun."

"So, Libby, you are not British born. Your lovely accent sounds so original."

"No, actually, I have come home after many years. I grew up right here in town."

"Oh, lucky you! I came here with my husband, Katy's father, when Katy was only two. He died and now Katy and I are grateful to be here among people who feel like family. I saw the need for a bakery and the rest is history."

28

"Such a lovely idea. When I was a kid there was one but it was pretty basic. White bread, blueberry muffins, oatmeal cookies and such but your wide variety of offerings is so appreciated."

Finally, it was time to return to work. "Well, Katy and I managed to clear a space that will accommodate the new service counter but getting there meant hauling out about a half ton of dirt, sand, bits of probably food and dead mice. Not to mention enough mouse droppings to build a mile long wall. Now for the next step."

Katy turned to her mother. "I cannot wait until we get to the books, Mom. While we were cleaning Libby told me things like how I must be very, very careful when handling the old books. Mice will have nibbled on the edges of the covers, especially the leather covers. You see, Mom, leather attracts mice because it came from an animal. In addition, over time leather grows brittle and can easily crack and break. When a binding breaks, naturally, the book can be ruined so, of course, you must be very careful when opening one of these old books or you could destroy its value. As Libby said, 'No sensible dealer opens a book widely because the binding could crack.' So, remember that, Mom."

Carrie lovingly patted her daughter's hands that were still looking grubby although she and Libby had used a special hand cleaner. "Well, sounds like you have found your niche in life, at last my darling daughter."

Turning to Libby, "She read *Little Women* at age four. Since then, she has been a dedicated bookworm. I am so pleased that you hired my angel and that she is proving herself to be a help with what looks to be an overwhelming project, Libby.

"Ah, bookworm meets bookworm. Sounds like we were destined to meet, Katy. That was my name in school here in town. Was proud of the moniker then and still am. Two of kind, eh, Katy?" Katy grinned widely.

"Got to get back to work. The witch is holding down the fort."

"Carrie, do you mean old Winifred the Witch of Barnstable? Oh, I should not use that derogative term, so sorry."

"No, really, she is proud of it. I met Winifred soon after my husband died and she told me things about life and death and love and so much more that helped me to move forward at a time when I was deeply depressed and feeling broken. She is so misunderstood. Kids love to think that she is like the typical Halloween witch but she will tell you that she is a Druid reincarnated from ancient times, endowed with special powers. Some day you should talk to her in private and she will tell you things that will take your breath away. Things about yourself and your destiny and such."

"Well, that's a whole new perspective. Thanks, Carrie. I hope to follow your advice…should I ever find the time. Let's go, Katy, back to the grind."

"Bye, Mom thanks for the lunch."

"Ditto, Carrie. Drop by anytime."

As they reentered the shop, Libby heard something. No, she corrected herself; *that was not a human voice, just the wind.* Turning to pick up the brush she used to carefully dust old books, there it was again. *"Welcome to my world. Neither dust nor grime nor time sullies the heart."*

SIX

The town of Barnstable was originally named Mattakeese. Prior to European colonization, Yarmouth was inhabited by the Wampanoag, an Algonquian people. In the Wôpanâak language the area was called "Mattacheese". Wampanoag tribes living in Yarmouth at the time of European settlement included the Pawkunnawkuts on both sides of the lower Bass River, the Hokanums in what is now northeastern Yarmouth, and the Cummaquids in what is now western Yarmouth.

The Cobb's Hill Cemetery was begun by one of the earliest settled families In Barnstable. Henry Cobb was active and useful in promoting the temporal, and in ministering to the spiritual wants of the first settlers. He was a town officer, a member of the most important town committees, and a deputy to the Colony Court in 1645, 1647, 1659, 1660 and 1661. On the 14th of April, 1670, he was chosen and ordained a ruling elder of the church in Barnstable, an office which he held until his death in 1679. In the government of his town and Colony Henry Cobb took a modest, yet not unimportant, part. For many years he represented Barnstable at the General Court at Plymouth. There were two deputies from the town. ... There can be no question but he was a man of standing and importance, valued and respected by his associates."

"Uncle, do you believe the stories about that Cobb guy who supposedly cursed his neighbor because his land flooded and drowned a bunch of his cows?

Stephen Crocker stood by the sign just inside the gate of the Cobb's Hill Cemetery that greeted visitors with a short history of the Cobb family for whom the cemetery was named. For a boy so young, only twelve, his interest in history, particularly of the place where he lived, surprised his family members. As young as he was, Stephen was allowed to join the Committee to Commemorate the First Ever Settlers in Barnstable. This group succeeded in adding the first paragraph on the sign that recognized the indigenous peoples who came there long before the white settlers.

Stephen loved helping his grandfather with the upkeep of the cemetery grounds on the Millway on Saturdays when the weather was clear and they could start early trimming trees and bushes, sweeping the paths and taking away the blackened dead flowers. "Never until they have fully rotted and not a healthy petal or leaf remains."

When he was first given this instruction, Stephen asked why. "As long as there is a hint of life remaining, Stevie boy, we leave those flowers in place. Folks bring flowers to gravesites because they represent life. Something alive and lovely to commemorate the life of those gone to whatever there is beyond this mortal coil deserves our care and respect."

One of the things Stephen loved about being with his grandfather was his use of old phrases and words no one used anymore except in the books he read from the library, from the huge town history section.

"So, what do you think Gramps, about curses? Maybe back then those kinds of things, you know, like ancient medicines people made from stuff like burdock and yarrow and that kind of stuff worked and time changed all that."

"Hogwash, boy. I know you like reading that kind of thing but take my advice and do not let it screw with your head. Beliefs are what change, not reality. Unfortunately, people get stuck. Some folks find comfort in hanging onto such balderdash. That's why religions are popular. Easier to believe silly made up stories meant to brainwash folks to make them easier to control."

"But there are some people in town, people you know and respect, Gramps, who do believe that if you come into the cemetery late at night and stand by Henry Cobb's grave, strange things happen. That guy who died, the one who owned the pink bookstore…he told me about it."

Gramps shook his head and continued sawing at the oak branch that hung too low, touching the top of a tall headstone. "Look Stevie, that guy was a nutcase, a real jerk who liked scaring people who came into his shop. He thought it helped the image and he sold more books if people thought he knew real stuff. Weird stuff. Damned fool lived in a bubble of his own making, he did. Looking forward to seeing how his niece does business there. Met her when she was shopping at the general store and she seems nice. Sensible and rational. Pretty, too. Come on, lots to do today, gonna rain like hell tomorrow."

"But Gramps, the witch told me the story of how that Cobb guy's neighbor whose name was Matthew Winslow took down lots and lots of evergreen trees between their two pastures and that allowed the water to build up and finally overflow onto his neighbor's land. Cobb had his pasture full of cows and they all drowned because the trees that had been there to drink the ground water were gone. So, Cobb cursed Winslow and forever after they were enemies, always fighting about things in public. The witch says that the pink bookstore is on that land where he once grazed his cattle and so the building is cursed."

"Damn, cut my finger. Get me a plaster will you son? Right there in the tool box."

That ended the one way conversation for that day.

SEVEN

When Ben met Libby coming down the street by the courthouse, her enthusiasm brightened his day. All morning, he had been in court dealing with a difficult divorce but seeing how excited she was about reviving the shop and the upstairs apartment lifted Ben's spirits. It was clearly obvious that Libby did not regret returning to her old life.

It has ceased to surprise him how many of his classmates had eventually returned to raise their families in the town. How well he recalled most of them swearing that once they got off the "boring" Cape they would never come back. He had never been tempted to leave, wanted nothing more than to get through college and then return to begin his grownup life. Fortunately, he chose the law at a time when finding work in his hometown had been easy. The space over the post office on Main Street, his first office, provided him with a front window looking out over the town. However, most important was the view of the courthouse where he tried his first case. Out the back window he could see Mattacheese Wharf on lovely Barnstable Harbor and, across the bay, Sandy Neck with its little cottages sitting proudly hugging the water's edge on the white sand spit of land jutting out into the bay. As a kid he wanted to live at the Sandy Neck lighthouse when he grew up. Well, at least he could gaze out of his office window at it now. He never regretted settling where he grew up and he hoped that Libby would not regret her decision to return home.

"Oh, Ben I have been having such a good time choosing paints from the New England colors in the Benjamin Moore paint collection, like this one." Pulling a paint sample sheet from her pocket, she held it out. "Nice, isn't it. It's called Phippsburg Blue. For the woodwork. White for the walls, of course…to brighten the place It is rather gloomy however, I suppose my uncle thought that gloom was in character for that type of shop. Oh, and I bought a lovely blue and white striped rug and a navy blue sofa with white piping at the second hand shop in Hyannis."

"You are absolutely sure you do not want to find a nice house, nearby but close enough to the shop rather than live in that cramped space?"

"Well, surprise, surprise. Matt Wentworth, the carpenter who did the work on the new offices in your building came by and found that Grover was not using all the space available. No, there is a large space at the back of the building that he might have expanded into but never did. It was blocked off by a large credenza full of junk. I swear, my uncle must have collected weird useless things at the dump and brought them home as if they were collectibles. Stuff like empty motor oil cans, one rubber boot, a bunch of rusted tools and well, just junk. Now, I can have a larger living room and a sizable bedroom. So there!"

"Congrats, Libby. Out with the old and in with the new. You are the best thing that ever happened to the old building. So happy for you." Ben curbed the urge to reach out and ruffle Libby's lovely hair, to lean down and place a kiss on her soft lips…*in front of God and everyone*, as his grandmother was wont to say about doing anything untoward like public displays of affection.

35

EIGHT

Change is good Libby told herself sitting by the window of the guesthouse in Osterville where she was staying until she could renovate the second floor of the bookshop. She and Ben had enjoyed a lovely lunch. The food was excellent and Ben, as always, was an interesting conversationalist. He told her about his first case fresh out of law school. They laughed at his mistakes, and, as he explained it, "I thought I was certainly the Perry Mason of Barnstable however as it turned out, I was more like Deputy Dog."

"Oh, my goodness, my grandmother used to talk about a long ago television show whose main character was an attorney named Perry Mason. Is that who you aspired to be Ben?"

"According to my mother, she watched re-runs of that old show when she was pregnant with me and that was when she decided that I too would grow up to be a lawyer. Can't imagine what my life would be like if she modeled my future on say, re-runs of The Jackie Gleason Show."

The thing that impressed Libby most about this new professional relationship that had quickly grown into a trusting friendship was how much the two of them laughed together.

After dessert, her very favorite, ginger crème brulée, she asked the question that had been gestating in her brain since she found out about the inheritance from her unknown uncle.

"Why do you suppose Grover Cobb decided to look me up and leave me the shop when he had a son to leave it to? After all, they could not have been so much at odds as father and son that it prevented Grover from leaving his house to him so why not the business, as well?"

"Ah, well, you have yet to see the house. My guess is that the old man never forgave his son and leaving him the house was a sort of twisted joke. The place is in terrible condition. It would take a fortune to restore it to its original condition. I could give you a tour if you like. I have a key only because Heather Michaels the appraiser invited me in to see the place when she took the original tour after the will was read. She insisted that I keep the key saying that she would never set foot in the place again. She looked almost panicked."

I think I can recall exactly what she said. 'Ben, there is something bad there. Not just the dirt and mice droppings that look like a thick black carpet but something…okay, get ready to give me a hard time…something ominous and really scary.' I didn't know what to say so I simply took the key and that was that."

"Oh my, did you share her odd feelings when you accompanied her there, Ben?"

"Yup. Understand this Libby; I am not the type to pick up on such things. Actually, I think that hauntings, if that's what you call it, are the products of a troubled mind. Yet, the place does feel…creepy."

"Creepy in what way?"

Ben laughed. "Look, I really do no subscribe to such things as ghosts and things that go bump in the night but walking through that house felt…damn, like the place was warning me that I had better get the hell out or else. I feel a fool talking about it but I felt something there."

"Hm. Think I will skip the tour, Ben. Thanks, anyway."

"How about giving me a peek at your improvements so far at the shop. If you ever need a hand on a weekend I can wield a paintbrush quite well. I can even manage a hammer and screw driver where needed. Oh, I forgot to ask how Katy is doing."

"Oh, Ben, she is terrific. Not only in the overwhelming job of cleaning old books with tender care but she jumps in and takes on anything that needs doing." Drop by on Saturday. Carrie comes by with hot muffins at eight. I think she is trying to fatten me up."

37

NINE

"Good morning. My name is Dr. Seth Magus. Thank you for having me as a guest speaker where I was never a student. I thought about Harvard however, I chose MIT. The cafeteria food was better and access to the river more direct.

"I have been asked to speak to you about my research into arachnology. For those who cannot abide the many-legged wonders to which I have devoted most of my life, the doors are open and awaiting your departure. Why would anyone want to study spiders is a question I get often. Here is my story, the story of how I came to be not only interested in but fond of spiders.

"When I was a boy, my father first owned a pub on Cape Cod. Then, for reasons I shall never know and never learn as he and I were never close and as he recently shipped out to Hades, he bought a bookstore. Rarely did I enter those dusty doors, walk across those musty rugs, or, I am happy to say, spend even one hour there keeping him company. Albeit, on the rare occasion when I did visit the old building that had experienced assorted incarnations I met my first black widow spider, my very first *Araneae* friend. For those of you who have spent your lives elsewhere and have been too busy and/or lacking in the penchant for visiting Cape Cod I shall enlighten you. Cape Cod is the eastern peninsula of Massachusetts, named by the explorer Bartholomew Gosnold in 1602. Having caught a large number of cod in the vicinity and obviously lacking in imagination, he dubbed it the Cape of Cod. Otherwise, it might have ended up being named for the indigenous peoples he encountered, the Mashpee Wampanoags. Of interest to anyone in the audience bemoaning the extinction of native fish due to overfishing, good old Gosnold noted in his logs that sailing the waters around the peninsula required great navigational skill due to the fact that the cod were so thick that a bucket plunged into the water never failed to come up full to the brim. The bow of his ship literally plowed through codfish, if we are to believe his notes.

"Ah, but you all have come here today to hear about spiders not codfish. There are those who would insist that deadly poisonous spiders can only be found in the desert, in dusty deserted old houses or barns, or possibly long deserted vehicles. Said creatures napping, awaiting a stupid invader's final, fatal foray into its silken web being a common image in children's stories and cheap thrillers, I am here to report that such is not the case. Well, not the whole story. As a curious boy growing up on that sandy arm, bent slightly at the elbow, its paw pointing northeast as if giving fair warning that it is the Nor'easters that threaten its existence every winter, by age four, all of this was irrelevant to me once I met my first charming, intriguing *Geolycosa pikei* the Cape Cod Wolf Spider. Only much later did I learn of the surprising variety of spiders to be found in the beach environment of Cape Cod, including both poisonous and nonpoisonous varieties that are indigenous to the peninsula. It would be a grave mistake to assume that deadly spiders exist only in caves in the west or lurk in rotting ante-bellum mansions in the south.

"Look closely and you will find that Massachusetts boasts its fair share of northern *Latrodectus variolus*, and southern *Latrodectus mactans* black widow spiders. Even today, it surprises visitors to the Cape that this historically charming, tourist-welcoming spit of land is home to nearly as many dangerous spiders as one might find say in Africa or India. Yes, in among the dunes, up in the maples and oaks, lurking in the bayberry bushes and possibly under a mattress in an inn that was once home to a sea captain and his family expect to come across a black widow spider…"

Sounds of astonishment from the audience.

"Ah, so now I have your full attention. No more napping for you dilettantes who spent the night in the local bar or brothel…or both, rather than boning up in preparation for this lecture." Around the nearly full lecture hall that can accommodate up to 492 came laughter, sighs, whispers and whistles. One woman shrieked, rose from her seat and walked swiftly out of the hall as if she had discovered one of these dreaded arachnids on the seat. Seth was in his element now.

Seth Horace Cobb, aka Magus, removed the pocket watch from the left hand pocket of his vest, gazed at it and sighed. While at Tabor Academy as a youth, already fully aware that one day in the near future he would be a world renowned Arachnologist, he decided that what he wore in future would be nearly as important as what he knew. After spending his freshman year at Barnstable High School, he begged his mother to enroll him in a private school where, he earnestly believed, he would be among "special boys and brilliant instructors" as was his due. Because she did not have the money, she appealed her son's case to a wealthy friend who came through both with tuition and a fine wardrobe from a prominent men's clothing shop in Boston. Unfortunately, the friend died before Seth was accepted for early enrollment at MIT in his junior year at Tabor, and the boy had no choice but to go begging to his father for the necessary tuition.

His father laughed in his face, leaning close enough so that Seth could smell the stink of his bad teeth and cheap whiskey. "I am not your father, bastard boy. Get the hell out of here."

Fortunately, MIT came through because of Seth's exceptional grades and his off the scale college board scores. Despite his success in his chosen career, running his own lab, and owning a gracious house on Beacon Hill in Boston, beneath his seemingly impenetrable crust and anti-social obnoxious arrogance there still lay a very broken boy.

Seth tapped the edge of the lectern and coughed in a way that spoke louder than any words could. *Time to turn all eyes back on me, inferior thinkers,* and he continued. "I was invited here to share with you details of my work with, to use their common name, spiders. Before moving on to my extremely valuable research let me add a few names to the list of nasty fellows one might encounter while walking the vast dunes of Provincetown or picnicking on a white sand bayside beach in Brewster. The Burrowing Wolf Spider and the Jumping Spiders of the family Salticidae, particularly the species Platycryptus undatus, have been observed on Cape Cod. The Nursery Web Spider, Pisaura mirabilis, lives on Cape Cod. Nursery web spiders are large, sometimes up to three inches. This oddly dubbed spider is named for the protective web the female spider weaves to enclose her babies and their egg sac. Ah, now that you have been spider enlightened does this news negatively affect your Cape Cod vacation plans? Actually, all of the aforementioned spiders are to be found all across the state of Massachusetts. My focus on the Cape comes from my childhood adventures in search of these elegant creatures for study. Yes, although everyone out there will not agree, spiders are the most spectacular creatures ever to appear on the earth. Ah, with the exception, of course, of the stinging, extremely poisonous *Pater noster, qui es in cælis*."

The atmosphere in the hall, that had certainly hosted its fair share of officious speakers down through the decades, felt thick and sticky. As one of the students put it later, "I felt as if I were caught in a spider's web. My entire body felt sticky and stiff, like a dead fly in a web. Shit, the man somehow hypnotized us into feeling that way."

In the front row, James Elliot, professor of entomology fidgeted in his seat. Unable to hold it in any longer he leaned toward his friend Arthur Sedgewick, known to his friends as "Sedge" and whispered. "Damn it, Sedge, had you met this asshole before you invited him to bore us all to death? If I remember my Latin, *pater noster, qui es in cælis* can only be a reference to his father who is in hell."

"Damn it Jim, I had no idea of what he was like. I know and greatly admire his work but he is indeed a damned troubled man. He might know his arachnids but give us a break with the god damned father issues. The arrogance of the man."

Around the hall people whispered, oblivious to the speaker or the courtesy expected of them in such a situation. Magus grew red in the face.

Sedge gazed around the hall. Although not pleased with the lack of respect shown by the audience he clearly understood it and knew that it would be useless to try to do anything about it. After all, what could he do? Jump onto the stage and demand better manners? Remind those in attendance that the speaker had the floor and that their behavior was deplorable? Damn it, the guy *is* an asshole, he told himself, what else can be expected of people who came to learn something new, perhaps, at least to hear a different perspective from someone who had been

41

receiving such praise in his particular field. Instead, he is more interested in making the audience feel stupid. God damned know it all bastard.

Like a beehive, the hall buzzed as people rose and left, not bothering to keep their voices down. A man and a woman passing by Sedge's seat were commenting on how disappointed they were after such an exciting build-up. "I really expected to learn something new from the guy; instead he obviously came here to try to show us all what idiots we are and what a genius he is."

Increasingly, attendees left the hall, some whispering but most purposely voluble, making no effort not to be heard making critical comments about the speaker.

Sedge sat, wondering what to do but unable to decide how to handle something so unusual. "Damn it all, Jim, I had no idea of what a jabbering idiot he is. His work has been receiving such high praise in the field. I read his last report on his work into figuring out what arachnid studies have failed to come close to in all the decades dedicated to this complex problem. He promises to have the answer to the age old problem that has frustrated those who hope to find the answer to spiders' *post-spin technique*."

On the stage, Magus grew red in the face. Then, the itch began. From head to toe, feeling like a billion tiny spiders intent on devouring every inch of his skin, the itch raced as it had for the past six or seven months ever since he found that special spider. The one that would finally make him worldwide famous, recognized for his genius, a god in his field. He had been absolutely confident that he would accomplish what no one had come close to doing. Isaac Newton, who dabbled in spider studies for his own enjoyment, wondered about the simple water spider an eight-legged marvel that can speed across water when threatened. Moving with lightning speed-for a spider, although its body configuration ought to make this impossible the water spider defied reason and gravity. Like a jet engine that forces burned fuel backwards to move the plane forward, in what is known as action and reaction, the laws of motion seem not to apply to the water spider. No animal, human or

42

otherwise, has ever managed to walk on water and yet the little spider that does not fly literally walks on water. The fisher spider (*Dolomedes triton*), a pond-dwelling species found in much of North America, is one of about 15 spiders that can do this, despite defying all the logic of science..

For months, Seth Magus did not leave the lab for days on end. Once this ancient secret that had frustrated so many scientists was revealed to him he would win prizes and be showered with praise for his exclusive genius. Post-spin would prove to the world that Seth Magus is the greatest mind in science ever.

Now, if only he could cure this terrible malady that seemed to be working to destroy him physically. His skin burned as if he'd been doused in gasoline and set afire. Nothing soothed the burn once it began. Stress brought it on. As he watched and listened to the audience as they left their seats laughing and grumbling, he felt his blood pressure rise, his throat began to close, his eyes blurred and he wanted to scream. He wanted to shout at the ignoramuses who could not possibly understand the importance of his work. Even at Harvard he had to deal with fools who treated him like a pariah. Just wait, fools, just you wait!

Whenever Seth encountered anything unexpected, a new barrier in his work that refused to give way, a colleague who questioned his results, or anything that challenged his authority over the subject that he considered his private property the itch raced over his body. Rarely did he invite anyone into his lab. He had no friends and never attended meetings of others studying arachnids. Seth Magus had no intention of sharing anything with anyone else for fear that they would steal his magnificent work. Particularly not until he had completed his studies on this his finest work. For months he had holed up in his lab, forgetting to eat and sleep. Now, having perfected his greatest work to the point where no one could possibly challenge him, he was ready to go public.

Not that he had intended that this was the time and place. No, this was simply an opportunity to show off to a Harvard audience. To rub his brilliance on the noses of students

43

and faculty of that haughty institution that would wish it had grabbed him sooner than had MIT.

Wanting to run himself, to exit the stage, the building and Cambridge, to fly away on wings of outrage, instead he could not move. His legs gave way. Slumped against the lectern Seth groaned.

Sedge stood, unsure of whether to go to the man or call for help. The hall emptied. Silence. Professors Elliot and Sedgewick waited, unsure of what to do next when suddenly Seth shouted at the top of his lungs.

"Imbeciles. You will regret this day. You will come running to me with praise. Just wait!"

"We need the guards to remove him. He's not going on his own."

Jim headed for the lobby to summon help. Turning, Sedge saw a man sitting in the very rear of the hall and quickly recognized him as Wesley MacIntosh, science reporter for the Boston Globe. Unsure whether this was good or bad for the school, all he knew was that it was too late to stop the news coverage.

Waiting for the guards, Sedge slowly approached the stage. "Dr. Magus," he spoke softly, hoping to relax the man who he now pitied. Noticing how red Seth's face and neck and hands were he wondered if this signaled a heart attack or stroke. Certainly, the man was incapacitated. Then, two men in dark suits, one entering from either side of the stage, saying nothing, moving slowly, reached Seth. Wanting to fight them off, Seth could not bring the thought into action. Behind them two medics arrived with a stretcher.

Suddenly, as the straps were being closed around Seth's body, he shouted; "Soon, the Cobb Web will be known to all the world. Armies will go to war wearing the Cobb Web. Automobiles will be far safer because of the Cobb Web. Camping gear will protect campers from every kind of weather and even marauding bears…" Then, he passed out.

Everyone gone and the stage empty Sedge turned to face the reporter who had moved closer, standing just a few feet

44

away, looking as dazed as the professor, he spoke quietly. "Hell of an event, eh, Sedge?"

"I don't know what you are going to do with this story Wes, but let me say that I never met the man before booking him for today. I had no idea that he was…"

"I think the term might be, *completely bonkers*, Sedge."

They laughed. "Don't suppose you will be using that particular term in your story, Wes."

"No, probably not."

They shook hands and as MacIntosh headed for the door, Sedge thought about a double whiskey.

Over drinks later, Sedge and Jim shared their thoughts about the disastrous event. "So the guy has daddy issues, Sedge. Boo hoo… Well, if he does this everywhere he speaks there must be legions of moaning audiences left in his wake wondering why on earth anyone would let him speak, let alone allow the nut to come through the door."

"Well, it's over now. Next step, how to quell the aftermath." The two touched glasses.

TEN

The scream echoed around the shop, seeming to be everywhere at once. The empty shelves acted like an echo chamber, surrounding Libby with a blanket of fear, preventing her from moving momentarily. Then, she ran in the direction of the back room where she knew Katy was working.

Libby had been fully engrossed in her morning project of sorting books for the newly painted shelves behind the sales counter. Meant to catch the eye of any buyer who loves fine leather book covers she had selected the very best from Grover's collection and hers. Only the previous day the boxes had arrived from England. Although she sold the shop fully stocked, she had made the proviso that she would be keeping her special collection of antique books in excellent condition to be to be shipped to her in Barnstable.

"Katy are you hurt?"

All she could see was the young woman's back, arched as if prepared for battle. Moving closer she could not believe her eyes. "Are those bones?"

"Someone must have hidden an animal in here. I pulled the loose boards away and this is what I found Libby. Who would have done such a terrible thing? Oh, I hope it was already dead!"

Libby pulled Katy back and put her arm across her shoulders, feeling the tension there. "Don't touch them Katy. They appear to be very old. At least there's no rotting flesh. No stink. Whatever poor animal it was has been long dead. But how did it get in to die?"

"Wait." Katy broke away from Libby's comforting arms and leaned forward. She gasped, leaped up and raced toward the front of the shop, shaking all over. Libby raced after her, "What did you see, Katy?

"I don't think the bones are of an animal. I think they are human. I took an anatomy course last year. The leg bones look very, very human, Libby."

"What? Human. How can that be…oh, we have to call the police. You sit here and try to get calm and I will call."

"Hello, this is Elizabeth Kavanagh at the Cobb's Hill Bookshop."

"Oh, yes, I heard about the new owner. Welcome to town. How can I help you Ms. Kavanagh?"

"This is going to sound strange but we may have uncovered some human bones in the shop."

"Oh, my. Would you like someone to come by to check on that, Ms. Kavanagh?"

"Yes, that would be helpful."

"My name is Ellen. This is my first day as dispatcher. I will get right on it. I will send an officer. Human bones, eh? Wow!"

A man's voice "Hello, this is Officer Finlay. I am on my way Ms. Kavanagh. Are you alright?"

"Yes, we are fine. The bones have been here for some time by the look of them. No danger to us."

"I am on my way. Only take me two minutes. Just stay away from the find, do not touch them."

"Don't worry, that is highly unlikely. Thank you, officer."

Libby made a fresh pot of tea and then in case Officer Finlay was not a tea drinker, she made a pot of coffee. By then, Katy had recovered and she was coming up with various scenarios to explain the bones.

"Well, we know that old man Cobb was a real nut case. He could have killed a complaining customer. Wouldn't put it past the old coot."

"That might be a bit over the top Katy."

"So, he had a girlfriend and they had an argument and he killed her with the letter opener. Or, maybe someone fell and hit his head and died and the old man feared he'd be accused of hitting and killing the man so he stuffed him into the wall."

"Or maybe it was a pirate and he was killed by Hannah Screecham because he refused her the gold."

47

Katy's eyes narrowed. "What on earth are you talking about, Libby?

Libby laughed and it felt very good. Yes, there were human bones lying in state in the back wall of her shop however her choices were to become paralyzed with panic or laugh and move on. "So, no one ever told you the story of Hannah Screeham? I am surprised. Hannah lived on Grand Island now known as Oyster Harbors. She was a friend of pirates, perhaps even Captain Kidd. This was the 1600's and many people were involved in smuggling, piracy and privateering. Hannah was an independent business woman ahead of her time. She set up a deal with pirates to bury their gold for them on her land. The pirates paid Hannah with gifts of jewelry or bags of silver. She sometimes pushed unsuspecting crew men into the hole with the gold and…"

The police officer entered the shop to find the two women drinking tea and looking as if nothing untoward had happened there. "Hello, I am Sgt. Jim Finlay. Come to check on your bones." "Yes, so pleased to see you…Jim…Jim who stole my bike in seventh grade?" Jim blushed and Libby laughed. "It's okay, Jim. I forgave you when you returned it with a new tire." "So sorry, Libby, I was desperate at the time. If I hadn't gotten to the store for my mother's cigarettes she would have…well, she was not the world's best mother." "Never mind. Time to take a look at what Katy found in the back wall."

The three of them walked to the rear of the shop. "Damn, I was hoping it was a dog the old man disposed of. He hated dogs, you know. Well, no, this looks suspiciously like a person. Human bones. Good thing the store is not open yet. Don't touch anything, I have to get the experts here to bag these up and take them off for testing."

"Jim, do you recall anyone in town gone missing, any mysterious disappearance years ago?" Libby surprised herself by how calm she now felt. Strangely enough, she was thinking about what an attraction for the shop it would be if the bones turned out to be some historic figure. "Hey, maybe it's Hannah Screecham." Katy laughed and made a creepy sound.

Jim nodded slowly. "I remember that story but I don't think this building was here that far back. As I recall, wasn't she a friend of Captain Kidd? When was that?"

"The 1600's. You are correct, Jim. This place was not built until 1820. So, no luck there. Although Captain Kidd's bones would most certainly put this shop on the tourist map."

Libby leaned in a bit closer hoping to see something that might be a clue. Some article of clothing from long ago, perhaps. Even a shoe could provide a clue as to the date the body was stuffed behind the wall. "Any sign of a peg leg, Jim? Maybe a gold nugget."

Jim shut off his small but very bright flashlight and backed out of the hole.

"Step back, ladies. Do not want to disturb the crime scene. Leave this to the experts." Jim called the station and spoke to the dispatcher telling her what he found and that he would be back soon to help her write up a report to send it to the state forensic dept. "Let the boss know and tell him that I will evacuate the shop."

"May I offer you coffee or tea, Jim. Least I can do to reward your heroics."

"Watch it, Libby, I used to be shorter than you, but no longer."

"True. And, you carry a gun. Well, Jim, you did grow up to be a solid citizen despite stealing a cream filled donut at the bake sale my mother and I worked at for the fire department collection for a new truck. And, a chocolate bar from my Halloween collection bag."

"Damn, guess I will never live down those horrible crimes. Coffee would be great."

"Speaking of crimes, maybe this was not anything so sinister. Knowing my uncle, perhaps some old person with no family died of a heart attack in the shop and nutty Grover stuffed the body into the wall so as to avoid being accused of murder. No one missed the old man and..."

"You, Libby Kavanagh, should be writing mystery novels."

"Well, if not Grover then maybe long before he owned the shop. Back when it was a private home. Now, that could have been murder. I know my uncle was odd, even maybe a bit insane but a murderer, I don't think so."

"Well, that would be fun if we had a murder here. Oh, sorry, not that I condone murder, but maybe it was someone evil."

"Well, ladies, got to get back to discuss this with the Chief. Thanks for the coffee. Best coffee I ever drank, actually. Mind if I drop by every day for a cup, Libby?"

"No problem Jim, just as long as you don't bring your sticky fingers along."

Jim faked shame, his head on his chest and Libby and Katy laughed and walked him to the door.

"Oh, I almost forgot. I have to instruct you to leave the premises until this case is solved."

"Jim, no way. I live here. My business is here. No way am I leaving because some ancient bones have been found. That is absurd. What could happen? The bones stand up and attack us? So long, Jim. Let me know when the experts will be arriving."

Jim shrugged and left the store. "Okay, back to work. Katy, you stay out front and wait on customers and I will finish shelfing the books delivered this morning."

"Wait. We are opening today?"

"Yes, I just decided that we will. Things may be in a bit of disarray but all the grime is gone and anyway we may not see a soul. However, I am turning the sign around and let's see what happens. Maybe the bones are our good luck charm."

"Wow, Libby, you sure are cockneyed optimist."

"Dear Katy, I think it is *cockeyed* optimist. A line from a song in the musical South Pacific."

ELEVEN

"Well, Seth, Dr. Wentworth has given you a clean bill of health. You are ready to leave us. I have your release papers here." The doctor looked up from the papers on his desk expecting something, at least a thank you. Maybe a nod. Not that he was surprised; Seth Magus had been one of the most difficult patients Dr. Wentworth had treated in a very long time.

"He is determined to ignore the treatment, stubborn and aggressive by turns. Not that I haven't had difficult cases before however, Seth is…I guess I do not have a professional term to describe   the   man. Glad to see him go."

"Let us keep in mind that we are turning him back into society. Is he really ready for that, Dan?"

"Well, let me put it this way. There is nothing more we can do for him unless we put him in a padded cell and forget about him."

Dr. Sontag gave his associate a look that Dan Wentworth knew only too well. They had worked together for nearly two decades and yet Edward Sontag still misunderstood his colleague's form of humor.

"Just kidding, of course. We don't even have any padded cells so I guess we have no choice but to send him on his way. As they say, a tough nut to crack. Be assured, Ed, I would not have signed him out if I did not think he is okay to return to society. Hey, if we locked up every guy who is nasty, uncooperative, belligerent and obnoxious we'd have damned few to run the world."

Now, the doctor waited for some response. However. Seth simply gazed out the window as if he had not heard a word.

51

"As long as you take your medication faithfully and do not overly exert yourself emotionally you should be fine. Ready to return to your important work. What do you say to that?"

"Goodbye." Seth rose from the chair, turned, and headed for the door.

"Seth, if you do not want to return here you must follow these orders. Are we clear about that?" The doctor's voice rose, unsure if the patient had heard a word he'd said.

Silence. Seth opened the door and walked out, slamming it behind him.

"God dammit, the man is an asshole." The doctor closed the file and shifted it to the side of his desk.

"Everything looks so nice, Libby. So many people sent flowers it looks more like a flower shop than a bookshop. This is so exciting." Katy walked around the room straightening a book here and there on the shelves feeling proud of all the work she and Libby had done in the past two weeks. Now, it was opening day and her mother had arrived with the desserts set out on a handsome antique table they had found in the cellar covered in dirt and cobwebs.

"Could not have done it without you, Katy. So, did you make the right career move?"

"Oh, yes. I love coming to work here. Best move I ever made."

"Good. Best employee I ever had. Well, I guess we are ready. You may unlock the door to the newly refurbished Cobb's Hill Bookshop."

All day, the shop was filled with happy people. Book sales were excellent and everyone offered congratulations. Many commented on how unpleasant the former owner had been. "I love old books and this shop had the best of the Cape Cod specific books that I collect and yet old man Cobb was so antisocial." "You would think that the man would have learned some manners but he was simply nasty and arrogant." "Definitely not a people person."

When Katy closed and locked the front door at five she was grinning albeit tired. "That was so great. I answered so many questions I thought I might end up losing my voice but it held up. Everyone loved the shop, Libby. You have a success here."

"Looks that way. I was so surprised to meet so many people who I knew as a kid. They remembered me and my parents. Like coming home."

"Well, it was your coming home party combined with erasing the aura of years of ownership of the shop by a nasty, irritating, totally unpleasant man who no one liked."

"Thanks for today, Katy. You did a great job. Enjoy your day off. See you on Monday."

"Not yet. Let me help you clean up, Libby."

"No. I insist. You have done enough and I have all day tomorrow to straighten out and get ready for opening on Monday."

"Okay, but I think I should help."

Libby hugged Katy and walked her to the door. "Make sure to tell Carrie how everyone loved her food. Enjoy your sail tomorrow."

"Haven't been sailing for weeks, been so busy here. Oh, I don't meant that I would rather have been sailing, Libby."

"Go. Time for you to have some fun. You have been covered in dust and mold and spider webs long enough. Get out on the bay and be refreshed. Goodnight."

Monday morning Libby awoke early in her newly painted and decorated bedroom over the shop. The sun glistened through the tall windows that had been so dirty it seemed as if they might never release their grime. The white walls, the newly sanded and oiled floor, the new rugs, the curtains and the bed quilt had transformed the room magically, it seemed. A far cry from the dreary depressing room where her uncle had slept for so many years like a hermit unconcerned about the grime surrounding him. Now, it was easy to forget all that and just enjoy the transformation. No wonder, she thought, the man was nasty and weird. Libby could not imagine anyone being so self-punishing. How could her mother and her brother, who were brought up in a lovely house with kind and caring parents, have turned out so peculiar she wondered?

53

Anxious to get downstairs to the shop to do the final cleanup Libby jumped into a pair of denim overalls she found at the thrift shop. Everything had gone so well on opening day. Ben couldn't make it because he had to be in New York for an important meeting however he sent a telegram and flowers. Good old Ben. He promised to cook her dinner on Wednesday night at his house telling her that he was an excellent cook.

On the bottom step Libby stopped, transfixed by what she saw. She could not believe her eyes. Rubbing them as if that would alter the horrifying sight before her, she gasped and nearly lost her balance. She grabbed the railing, took one more step, and froze in place. *I am still asleep and having a frightful nightmare?* Pinching her arm hard, she knew she was wide awake and yet, how could the scene before her be real? No, this had to be her imagination…nothing like this could possibly be real.

Yet, it was horrifyingly, mind-numbingly real.

Everywhere, every surface, every shelf, the walls and everything in the shop was draped in cobwebs. Thick, hazy gray cobwebs, as if giant spiders had spent the night working to enclose the entire shop in their gauzy artwork, filled the scene before her. Moving slowly, not wanting to touch the webs but unable to move an inch without feeling them on her skin she moved forward toward the phone on the counter. Shivering, not from cold but from something akin to freezing, Libby dialed the old fashioned phone that she chose to keep because it fit the shop character, she dialed the police station.

"Good morning. Is Officer Finlay available?"

"Yes. Who may I say is calling, please?"

"Elizabeth Kavanagh from the Cobb's Hill Bookshop."

Jim arrived to find Libby standing outside the shop looking terrified. "Libby, are you hurt? What's wrong?"

"Oh, Jim, something awful has happened inside."

"Not another bunch of bones."

"No." Her voice quavered. "Something even scarier. Cobwebs everywhere."

Jim gave her a quizzical look and asked, "How about I go inside alone and check on things. Okay, Libby? You stay right here and try to relax."

Jim could not believe his eyes as he entered the shop. At first thinking that what he saw was a smoke-filled room, a fire smoldering somewhere, he figured that was what Libby had meant but the smoke had affected her mind. Had her fear confused her? When his eyes adjusted to the lack of light even though the day outside was brilliant, he could see them. Draped over everything were spiders' webs alright. But how could such a thing have happened? Moving further into the room as his uniform became draped in webs and he had to keep pushing the invading filmy stuff from his face, he could understand poor Libby's distress. He shivered.

Nothing he could do there, Jim returned to Libby who was sitting on the bench on the front porch. He had such a crush on her in high school. Always perfectly dressed, her long blonde hair always neatly encased in a thick braid that hung down her back, sometimes tied with a ribbon and sometimes with a scarf, he knew that she would never date him because she was tall and he was short. Now, her hair ruffled from sleep she sat in the sun wearing a blue and white bathrobe and fluffy slippers. Now, he was taller than she but somehow she was still way out of his reach. "Libby, are you alright?"

"Yes, thanks for coming. Guess this is way out of your normal routine. Can't arrest spiders for redecorating my shop."

"Libby, this is unbelievable in the extreme." Hoping to lighten the atmosphere, he laughed and said, "No one is going to believe my report. Probably send me to Boston for a psychiatric exam."

"I'd say we could keep it between the two of us but if I hire a local cleaner to take care of the mess our secret will be all over town in a short time."

"True. Do you have somewhere to go until the situation is cleared up? Hey, my old friend Maxine has a cleaning company down in Dennis. I could ask her to keep the secret. Would that work for you?"

"Thanks, Jim. Sounds like a plan. I can say that we had a leak or something and will open again as soon as it is fixed. I guess it is back to the inn for me for a few days. Damn, the opening was so great, now I have to close because a bunch of highly aggressive spiders reawakened from a deep sleep."

"Can they do that? Sleep for years, maybe centuries, and suddenly awaken and go to work…do you think?"

"No. Well, I am no expert on Arachne but it sounds unlikely to me. However, I am beginning to wonder about a lot of things that are highly improbable lately."

TWELVE

"Ben, it is totally unbelievable. How could it have happened? Oh, this is unreal in the extreme."

"Libby, I can be there in a few hours. I stopped to visit my mother in Connecticut but I am on the road again. Hold tight and do not touch anything, please. Go upstairs and read a book. I am coming. Damn it, first bones and now spider webs."

"I know. Makes a person wonder about the world beyond ours, doesn't it? Maybe my uncle cursed the shop…"

"Okay, no going off the deep end Libby. We will solve both riddles and all will be well."

"The place was so clean, Ben. Every bit of dust and mouse droppings gone, certainly we would have found spiders when we were cleaning. Not to mention that these aren't just a few stray webs we might have missed. This is a blanket of gauze that fills the entire shop, draped over furniture, covering books on the shelves and…"

"We can find an expert on spiders, Libby. There has to be a reasonable explanation. Probably a rare breed that multiplies rapidly and there was no way you could have known. Try to relax."

"At least the mess is only on the first floor so I can safely return upstairs…in fact, no need to go to the inn. I can use the back outside stairs. Yes, I would rather be here when the cleaners are here to oversee the job. Oh, the place was so clean and shiny. Damn, damn!"

"Hold tight, help is on the way. See you shortly. Have a nice cup of tea."

"Katy, no work today. There is a problem…." Sitting in the wing chair in her bedroom, still shaking from the shock of what she found downstairs, Libby is determined not to let it throw her. After Jim left she pulled her bathrobe up over her head and with just her eyes uncovered she had slipped across

57

the shop and out the back door. If she was going to depend on these stairs in future, they would need some work. She had ignored them because she did not need them but now their condition, shaky and encased in vines demanded her immediate attention. Thankfully, the angry spiders had not invaded the second floor. Her trusty electric kettle brought from Hastings allowed her to have her morning tea. Now, her nerves in better shape, she had to make plans, arrangements and changes.

"Katy, I would not blame you if you wanted to quit working here. Let's face it; bones and spiders' webs do not make for a charming work atmosphere."

"No way do I want to quit, Libby. I love all this mystery. Better than any of the mystery books I read. Do you want me to come in to help clean up the webs?

"Thanks, but no, this requires special professional cleaners, Katy. Jim has a friend from down-Cape who will do the job and keep our secret. Such weird happenings could affect our business. I will let you know when I am ready to reopen."

Ben stood out on the front porch calling. "Libby, are you up there?"

Now dressed and more relaxed thanks to two cups of English breakfast tea, Libby opened the window and leaned out. "Hi. Welcome to the haunted bookshop. Nice to see you. Come around the back Ben, the problem is limited to the shop itself. Be careful on the stairs."

THIRTEEN

Determined to quash all foolish thoughts about curses and ghosts and possibly murder, most of all that Uncle Grover's ghost came back to punish her for altering his shop, for trying to erase his memory, Libby headed out for a walk in the sunshine. The cleaners were scheduled for the next day so there was nothing she could do at the shop.

First human bones and now webs. Libby's mind roiled with confusing thoughts. She had expected a lot of hard work when she first saw the condition of the shop, of the entire building. Soon, it would need a new roof and possibly a new heating system. With any luck, she would begin making enough money to take a loan to bring the old building into proper condition. She had come to love the old place, quirky as it was. Pink was hardly her favorite color but when she suggested changing it she had received so many objections from town's people she knew that would be a mistake. Everyone knew the pink bookshop in Barnstable so she would have to grow to love it the way it was.

When the witch came walking quickly out of the post office as Libby was passing on her way to the harbor, the two collided. "Oh, so sorry, are you alright?"

The old lady straightened and smiled. "I am fine dear. Thanks for arriving."

"Pardon me, what do you mean? Arriving?"

"When two points in the universe collide, magic happens, my dear." Putting her arm through Libby's, steering her in the opposite direction from the harbor, the witch made a kind of purring sound.

"Now, I know what is happening at your bookshop. Have no fear, this kind of thing is but part of the plan."

People Libby knew from the shop opening and from her childhood passed by them as they walked and greeted Libby with friendly comments.

59

"Lovely opening celebration." "So pleased to have you back home." "Love what you have done to the old pink building." "Great to have the bookshop open again and friendly, Elizabeth." Her high school English teacher, Mrs. Goode, stopped them, patted the hand of the witch and hugged Libby. Libby clearly recalled how the woman began each class on the first day of school each year. "Now, children, I am Mrs. Goode and I am here to teach you good English."

As they walked on, Libby could not decide whether to extricate herself from the old woman everyone referred to as the Witch of Barnstable or simply let things evolve according to the old woman's whims. What could she have meant by *Part of the plan...*?

Allowing herself to be steered by the old woman, Libby found herself on a sandy path that she had never known was there, behind the general store. How could she, a kid who loved exploring and knew every inch of her hometown, not know about this, she wondered.

Stopping by a sizeable rock, the witch said, "This is where he buried the other one, dear. He rolled a large rock over the grave and since no one ever comes along here, everything is just as it was." Libby shivered despite the warm day.

"Are you telling me that my uncle murdered someone and buried the body here?"

"Yes, dear. He had many women. Once, he buried one at sea. Well, I guess that is not actually a burial however, that is the expression that explains dumping a dead body into the water, is it not?"

"So, my uncle Grover Cobb murdered these women and disposed of their bodies here and there. Is that what happened? Did no one miss these women and wonder where they had gone?"

"They were women from away, you see. Desperate for work and a place to live. They never strayed from the shop. Grover did not allow them to leave."

"I don't understand. My uncle kept these women as...prisoners."

"Oh, they agreed to the arrangement. He mesmerized them it would seem. Once, I met one of them when she crept outside to get some air on the back steps when I was picking blackberries. She said hello but when I came closer I saw that her eyes were odd. I think Grover stole their souls."

Libby's mind roiled. Too much crazy input. Had she slipped into an alternate universe where life emulates books? "So, you are telling me that no one knew these women were there and therefore, no one knew or cared when they disappeared. *Were murdered.*

"Well, dear, your mother knew."

Libby's mouth dropped and her heart began to race. Surely this old woman was only imagining, making up stories for the purpose of shocking her. She had to get away from her right now.

"Let me take you back to the road and you can return home. I have some business to attend to and..."Libby looked at her watch, "Oh, look at the time. I am late for an important appointment."

The old woman did not resist. They returned to Main Street. Libby said goodbye to her and turned to head toward the harbor, once again, anxious to be as far away from the crazy woman as she could manage. She considered running but knew that passers-by would react and think her odd. Over her departing shoulder the old woman croaked, "I will visit you very soon to show you where he hid the bones in your bookshop, dear."

Seemingly unable to hold back the words Libby blurted out, "No need, I already found them."

Libby stood on Mattacheese Wharf looking out at the sparkling blue water. A children's sailboat race was taking place and the sailors were raising spinnakers to run downwind. The salt air felt wonderful and it ought to be cleansing her mind of the crazy old woman's words but instead all she could think about was that her mother knew that her uncle was a murderer. No, not possible. Foolishness. Her mother was a good and honest and kind person, hardly someone to cover up for a brother who made a habit of killing women. The witch had to be wrong.

61

FOURTEEN

"Sir, you had five phone calls regarding the Cobb Web while you were gone. Such a great name."

"I do not need to hear your opinions, Mary Ellen, just do your job. Give me that list."

Seth grabbed the list and stormed into his office, slamming the door. The secretary was new, the sixth one in a year. If Seth was lucky this one might last because her father had been much like this officious man who seemed to be *"missing important human chips"* as she told her friends.

"Yes, I have been away on important business. No, I am not ready to share the information. When I am ready I will write it up and publish. In the meantime, do not call again."

Mary Ellen stepped into the office carefully, as if she were entering the cage of a vicious wild animal. "Sir, this mail just came. Would you like me to make some coffee for you?"

"God damn it girl, I do not drink coffee. How many times do I have to tell you that? Just put the mail here and get out. Go!"

Seth unplugged his phone and told Mary Ellen to take the rest of the day off. Anxious to write up his article for Science Magazine, he settled in to his writing on the Cobb Web. *Yes, it is a great name!* His life's work; the most important thing he had ever done and soon the world would know his genius and he would never be forgotten. What a tragic waste of time it had been being locked up, prodded, stabbed and most insulting of all, questioned about his sanity. Now, with the rash under control thanks to the doctors who figured out what caused it once he informed them of the spider bite, he could work without constantly itching.

What title to use? Well, he could decide that later. For now, he had to put the vital information into a tidy order. Everyone who has ever worked on the mystery of spiders' webs has been stymied about spiders' "post-spin." Although scientists have managed to produce spider silk with the biochemical integrity of other natural fibers, no one has managed to mimic a spider's ability to stretch the fiber in order to align the fiber molecules that result in increasing the fiber's amazing tensile strength. Until now. He had not only solved the ages- long mystery of post-spin, he had produced, even if only a few inches, a fabric that would astonish the world.

The words flowed onto the screen.

Spider webs are astonishingly strong. Spider silk has the tensile strength of up to 1.75 gigapascals (GPa), or over 178 kilograms per square millimeters in cross-section/392.4 pounds. As such, spiders are tiny silk production factories. The "thread" is stored as a highly concentrated liquid inside the spider's body. A common garden spider, for instance, is capable of producing as many as seven different types of silk. In addition: each type of thread serves a very distinct purpose. Among these vital purposes is the stretchiness of the silk. Another is making the thread less brittle. Other qualities instilled in the spider's factory are the production of proteins that protect the threads from bacteria and fungi and maintain sufficient moisture.

The engineering of silk has to do with the transmission of information through DNA. As compared to human engineering that depends upon using more and more energy to solve problems, the spider (Nature) does this through the use of better information.

Seth took a deep breath. His hands shook and his heart raced. Everything was perfect. Oh, if only his son of a bitch father was around to watch him become famous. Mean, selfish bastard. Ah, but he had succeeded in spite of the miserable fool.

FIFTEEN

Ben sat on the new couch in Libby's now bright and cheery apartment over the shop. "You must not believe the old woman, she is called a witch so that's clue enough to her insanity, Libby."

"Oh, Ben, if only you had heard her. She knows things. She knows about the bones in the bookshop. Everything she said, despite sounding like words right out of a cheap horror novel, somehow sounded as if they held some truth. Weird, distressing truth but nevertheless, I felt as if she knows things about Grover no one else knows."

"She likes frightening people. That's what the kids love about her. Well, the one's old enough not to be terrified out of their little impressionable minds, that is."

"What I am going to tell you, you must promise never to breathe a word of to anyone, Ben."

"I am your attorney, Libby. My lips are sealed."

"She told me that only my mother knew that he kept these women and that he killed them."

Ben laughed. "Sorry, but I knew your mother. She was the kindest, sweetest and most rational person around. She would never have covered for that nut of a brother. She hated him! Can you imagine her covering for a murderer brother? Come on, Libby, the witch played you good."

Libby refilled their teacups and then stood looking out the newly cleaned window overlooking the back garden. She had such great plans for the overgrown space come spring. Flowers for the shop and vegetables for her table. Her mother always had terrific productive gardens. Her dear, sweet mother…

"By the way, I got the report on the bones. If you are too upset to hear it I can wait until a later time, Libby."

Libby sat in the wing chair and smiled. She hoped the smile looked genuine although it was only surface quality.

64

"Let me have it. Now or later the news will hardly astonish me after time spent with the witch."

"Well, the bones are human. Probably been in the wall for forty or so years according to the forensic pathologist."

"Male or female?"

"Well, sorry to say, but they are definitely female. Damn."

Libby shot him a look loaded with *I told you so.*

"How do they know that? I mean, I have always wondered how the sex of bones can be determined." Ben finished his tea and poured himself another cup. Always a coffee man, Libby had converted him with a tea laced with cinnamon (he loved cinnamon toast).

Libby smiled genuinely. "Well, my dear friend, if you read more mysteries with modern day forensic science in them you would be privy to that fact. Modern forensic science is so fascinating. Do you know that from bones they can determine where the person grew up? The foods eaten in childhood and the water they drank as their bones grew stronger, contained microcosms that can still be detected, even long after death. How's that for amazing?" Libby anticipated Ben's next words.

"Isn't science grand? So much better than the words of a crazed old woman who calls herself a witch."

"Shall I continue, smart ass?"

"Please do."

"As to sexing the bones; that is easy. Female pelvic bones are the giveaway. They are quite different from those of the male of the species. You see, the female pelvis is broader and shallower. Otherwise, they would not be able to give birth."

"So, what about male bones, Libby? Are they bigger and stronger and full of bravado?"

"Actually, it is something called the nuchal crest that is the giveaway. Also known as the occipital crest, this area, where the muscles from the back of the neck attach to the base of the skull is smooth and rounded in females but hooked and protruding in males."

"Wow, you do know your stuff." Ben clapped his hands and grinned at Libby.

"So, our bones are female. Hm, so the plot thickens as they say, Ben."

"Well, let's see. Forty years ago in Barnstable would be around 1976. Any special memories of that year, Libby?"

"Since I was yet to enter this world, no memories."

"Guess we will need witnesses, people who were in town at that time, in particular those who knew your uncle."

"Considering of course that no one knew him well since he kept to himself and when out in public he was totally obnoxious. Hardly qualities that would attract friends. Oh, if only I knew how much my mother actually knew about her brother's life. For instance, if he happened to have the peculiar habit of murdering his girlfriends. I know!"

"Pardon me, Libby. You know what?"

"I know the perfect person to ask about this. Abby Dunne. She is still alive. I have been meaning to visit her. She was my mother's very best friend. If anyone knows, Abby does. Is she still in her home?"

"Still in her house on the marsh, as far as I know."

SIXTEEN

"I will be in the lab all day, Mary. The phone will be off the hook so don't bother trying to reach me."

"My name is Mary Ellen, sir."

"What?"

"You called me Mary, sir."

"Whatever."

Behind his back the young woman made a face.

In the lab Seth carried on conversations with his spiders. This was the day he would carry out his final test before submitting his article to Science magazine and his report to the company who would be paying him a fortune for his work. Soon, the fabric made from his experiments that will be far stronger than Kevlar and perhaps become a glass that is bullet proof will make him world famous. *Take that Grover Cobb you mean bastard. Your son will be world-renowned despite your ignorance and arrogance.*

As he worked he recalled his latest out of lab experiment and how very well it had gone. No one suspected him, although once his success became public knowledge he just might make a visit to the scene to brag. How he would have liked being there that morning when she viewed the magnificent beauty his little friends had produced overnight. Smiling, he spoke aloud.

"Thanks to you she will live in fear that it will happen again. Next time, however, we will employ the stronger web, the soon to be world famous Cobb Web. Have no fear, my talented friends, of course I will find a way to be there to watch as she becomes entangled…as the breath is squeezed out of her. To hear her last tortured breath, to see her face turn a lovely shade of plum, to hear her final strangled words.

Then, everything will be mine…as it should be."

SEVENTEEN

"Thanks so much for seeing me Abby."

"Oh, my dear, so pleased to have you back in town. I do not get out much these days but I did intend to visit you at the shop eventually. How are things going, dear?"

"Very well. We had a lovely opening and I have high hopes for the business now that the place is far more inviting. My uncle did live and work in a rather filthy situation. Well, he seems to have respected the books and dusted them on occasion but the building was in terrible shape. All fixed now however. I would love to have you visit."

"Your parents would be so proud. That Grover Cobb was a terrible man. Unfriendly, mean and well, just not a nice man."

"I know. As I recall, my mother cut off all communication with him at one time. Do you know if she ever reunited with him?"

"Well, I am not sure that reunited would be the word I would use but she did do something that surprised me."

"Oh, what was that?"

"Just before Christmas each year she visited him. She did not let your father know this, however. He was very protective of your mother and he surely hated Grover for his obnoxious behavior toward the family."

"I didn't know that. Why would she decide to do that considering that supposedly she had nothing more to do with him after they had that huge falling out?"

"Your mother was a lovely woman who loved her family and friends and I know it was difficult for her having a brother like him. Even as a boy he was mean. He hurt animals. You know what an animal lover your mother was, dear. It broke her heart and he seemed to enjoy her misery. He would bring her animals he had killed. All bloody and twisted limbs…Oh, I…"

68

Libby moved from the chair to sit beside Abby. She hugged her and comforted the woman who seemed as if she might faint.

"No more. Tell me no more Abby. I cannot bear to see you like this. Let's just change the subject. I had a lovely man visit with a huge collection of Cape Cod books his father collected. I bought the lot. Can't wait for you to check them out."

Abby pulled herself together and smiled. "Dear, dear Libby, the man is gone and good riddance and you are the owner of the shop so let's celebrate. There is some brandy in that decanter on the desk. Glasses in the kitchen cupboard. If you wouldn't mind, once I am seated, getting up is, well, I am no spring chicken anymore."

Going for the glasses Libby recalled that although her mother and Abby were not the same age. Abby was quite a bit older and yet they were great friends who both loved playing golf, hunting for antiques and reading British mysteries. Unfortunately, both of Libby's parents had died far too young.

Carrying two brandy decanters back into the sitting room Libby thought about her mother's deception. How strange that she would have kept such a secret, stranger still that despite having broken off all connections with her nasty brother that she went to wish him happy holiday.

The two ended their visit with a promise to do it again, the following week. Libby would pick up Abby and give her a tour of the shop and then they would lunch at the Dolphin. Maybe then, Libby hoped, she could broach the subject of Grover's women friends…and the possibility of murder.

EIGHTEEN

"Yes, sounds lovely, Carrie. How about four dozen? No. I will stop by in the morning to pick them up. I have given Katy the day off. It's that lull in holiday shopping in the last days before Thanksgiving. Really slow here."

Having ordered cookies in the shape of turkeys for the children's party she arranged with the kindergarten teacher, her old friend Susan Hill, things were looking good. The shop was decorated and a table was filled with children's books set on Cape Cod. Libby was surprised how many books for children had been set on the Cape in the past few years. There would be storytelling and cookies and ice cream. Just to be sure, Carrie had agreed to make the treats with gluten-free flour.

Now, all Libby had to do was arrange the dolls dressed in period clothes loaned by a lovely woman who collects and repairs dolls. High enough so the children could not touch them with sticky hands but close enough for the charming details to be seen. Working with Susan had renewed their close friendship. Both of them being single, they had started attending theater productions and talks all around the Cape. Libby was delighted to find that it would be difficult for a person to plead boredom with all the things there were to do from plays, concerts, and art exhibits to amazing gourmet meals presented by local chefs usually accompanied by music by local artists. Thinking that she might miss all the culture in and around Hastings, this fall had proved that the town she grew up in, in fact, the entire peninsula had grown into a very special cultural scene.

Gently removing the dolls, one by one, from their padded case, Libby heard the door open. Well, she thought, the rare customer who needs a book for a holiday gift.

Turning, to look, Libby was pleased to see Abby standing in the doorway.

"Lovely day, isn't it dear? I have always loved Indian summer. Oops, do I now have to call it indigenous people summer?"

Libby moved from the shelf half full of charming dolls to hug Abby. "No, I think you are alright, everyone still uses the term. One of those accepted New England things."

"So festive in here, dear. Quite a difference from when Grover had the shop."

"Yes, I don't imagine my uncle threw holiday parties for children in his time."

"My, my no, if he had it would have been to roast and eat them like the big bad wolf."

The two laughed and Libby offered Abby tea which she said she would just love to warm her after her walk.

"Elizabeth…" Abby hesitated and Libby laughed saying, "Oh no, am I in trouble? Mother only called me that when I was."

"No, not at all. I had a memory late last night. Well, I do not sleep very well so sometimes I find myself lying there time travelling I suppose you would call it."

"Sounds interesting."

"Well, it can be. Last night I recalled something your mother said once around the holidays. I suppose that is why my mind pulled it out of storage."

Libby refilled their tea cups and waited to hear Abby's memory.

"I recall that once after she had visited her brother to wish   him   a   happy Christmas…you remember that she did this but your father did not know, right?"

"Right. You were the only one she told."

"Yes. Well, she and I were walking down on the beach one afternoon as we liked to do on sunny days, even in winter. As I recall, it was shortly after the New Year and she mentioned that every time she visited the shop a few days before Christmas, there was a different woman there with Grover."

"Do you mean, a different woman working there?" Libby wondered where this could be going.

"Well, she asked me if I knew any of the women he hired and I did not and, in fact, I had never heard anyone mention being waited on by anyone but Grover. Not that he did much business for many years because the place was so filthy and such. However, his collection of Cape Cod books remained a lure for collectors despite the unpleasantness of the shop and the owner."

"Did she say why she was interested in women he may have working here, Abby?"

"Well, she said that she had an odd feeling about these women. What she said was that they seemed either feebleminded or maybe drugged."

"Oh my, that's certainly a peculiar thing for my mother to say."

"I just thought you ought to know, dear. I cannot get the thought out of my mind that he killed a woman and hid her body in the wall here in the shop."

"I know. Officer Jim Finlay and the forensic people have been back here a few times digging around in there for evidence."

"Does it make you uncomfortable knowing that there were human bones right here in your shop, Libby?"

"Well, I suppose it kind of adds a kind of mysterious caché to the place, Abby. Too bad I do not feature crime novels."

"Well, better you than me, Libby. I think it would put me off my feed…and my sleep." Abby rose saying that she had some last minute food shopping to do. "My son Louis and his family are coming and each one of them has some kind of food fear or allergy or whatever. So, planning a menu is not fun. Have a lovely holiday, Libby."

Libby stood in the doorway both confused and fascinated watching Abby walk away. So, Uncle Grover may have had a drug problem and he hung around with women (had romances with women?) in a drugged state even during business hours. Why did no one know about these women was an important question. But, most important of all was the question: was Grover Cobb a murderer?

Children's happy voices filled the shop and Libby's dark thoughts flew away like dandelion fluff in a breeze. A few hours later, Libby's equilibrium was, once again, sent into a spin.

NINETEEN

When the phone rang Libby was filling an order for a customer who had called to ask if she had any books on witches and ghosts on the Cape. Into the box Libby placed William Simmons wonderful book, *Spirits of New England Tribes,* and a newly written book about Hannah Screecham called *The Witch of Grand Island.*

"Libby, hope I am not getting you at a bad time. Susan Hill told me you were hosting a kid's party."

"Hi, Jim. Party's over and everyone seemed to have a great time. Well, all except for one little boy who wet his pants and was very embarrassed. What can I do for you Jim?"

"Well, something strange has occurred." Officer Jim Finlay's voice, thought Libby, sounded more like Mr. Rogers from her favorite childhood show than a police officer who dealt with crime.

"And this strange occurrence will be meaningful to me because…? Did you recover a car trunk full of stolen books, perhaps?"

"Oh, I wish it was that simple, Libby. No, I found more bones."

While she waited for Jim to arrive at the shop to tell her the full story, Libby packed away the dolls. The children had loved them. The turkey cookies had been a big hit and Libby was very impressed with how Susan was with the children, particularly the poor little boy who got so excited about finding the secret prize hidden by Libby in among the children's book that he wet his pants.

When the door opened, Libby expected it to be Officer Jim but instead it was Ben.

"Hi. Heard the party was a great success. You sure have changed the atmosphere here as well as the shop's reputation. Everyone is pleased to have you here Libby."

"Have you talked to Jim, Ben?" Libby realized that she was shaking. Her hands felt tingly but she was determined not to let her fear show.

"Yes. I don't know what to say, Libby."

Jim entered the shop before Ben could say more.

"I need tea for this. You two help yourselves to the coffee machine. I'll just boil some water and be right back."

When Libby reentered the shop, Jim and Ben were seated in the reading area set in a corner that got excellent light from three tall windows. When she moved in she did now know that there were windows there because of shelving covering them completely. Who in their right mind, she asked herself, would cover up such lovely windows and deny the light to enter the shop?

Sitting, she could sense the tension. "Okay, so where were the bones this time?"

Jim leaned forward and spoke directly to Libby, his hands tightly clutching his coffee mug. "Well, some neighbors at your uncle's old house, well, Seth's house, complained about someone breaking in there. Turned out it was actually four people. Two men and two women. They broke a window and were sleeping there for a few nights. The neighbors waited to report it assuming it was your cousin Seth but when they spotted them leaving one morning they called the station."

"Ah, so they left behind some bones." Libby's attempt to lighten the atmosphere only worried her more than before. "Okay, so they found more human bones in the house and ran away terrified. No harm done."

"Not quite. I went there to check it out and found that they left behind food and paper cups and stuff from their stay. The place is such a mess it was hard to say whether they did any damage but I called Bill Simmons to board up the first floor windows after I talked to Seth who agreed to pay for the work."

"So, you spoke to my peculiar cousin, son of my peculiar uncle. How did that go, Jim?"

"Oh, he is weird, all right. Actually, he didn't seem to care what happened at the house. I told him that I could leave things as they are and let every homeless person on the Cape move in if that was alright with him. He could perform a needed public service. Sorry, not usually so flippant with people, but you know his voice is just so officious. Like father, like son, it seems."

"Please get to the bones, Jim. I am waiting with bated breath…whatever that really means." Libby gulped her hot tea and waited. What did her mother's words about strange women have to do with all this and why would there be bones in both the shop and the old house that her uncle bought and never lived in?

"While I was there I took a look around, just in case. Upstairs in what looked like a bedroom I accidently bumped into a rusty old bedspring leaning against a closet door. The spring fell and the door followed. Inside…"

Ben leaned forward now. He reached over to put his hand on top of Libby's gripping the arm of the chair. He could feel her shivers and he wanted to take her in his arms and make it all right for her.

"Inside were bones. White, chalky looking bones just like here in the wall. Forensics has them and we should hear by tomorrow. Oh, by the way, Kelly at the lab explained that dating bones can be somewhat iffy. I mean the forensic people can be off by ten or so years, hardly a big deal but just for your information, the bones here could be as old as say, fifty years or only twenty-five to thirty. I only tell you this because from my end it helps to be able to fit the pieces together according to the likely timing. I mean, in checking women missing from town, dates are important."

"Of course, Jim." Ben looked at his watch and rose. "So sorry but I have to be in court."

"I have to get back to the station. Wish I hadn't had to upset you Libby. Leave this in my hands and don't worry. We will get to the bottom of it as soon as possible."

Libby walked to the door with the two men wondering if they would find answers to now two mysterious deaths or if they would remain in the unsolved mysteries realm forever.

"Oh, I must tell you what Abby told me. It might be important."

After she finished relaying the story of her mother's holiday visits to her brother, the brother she had virtually disowned except for these special visits each year, the men left and Libby stood breathing in the clean salt air.

Well, she thought, I suppose when the two mysteries are solved it will make some local writer happy. Nothing like a good local mystery to increase business. I could give tours and show people where the bones were found.

Her thoughts then went to Seth. No wonder he was weird with a childhood like his. Although his mother seemed to have done her best, still psychologists claim that boys need to be close to their father to develop a healthy psyche.

Perhaps she ought to reach out to her cousin. After all, they were all each of them had left of family. If his father turned out to have murdered two women, maybe more, he would need a friend, someone who could comfort him. Everyone said that Seth was prickly however, if she extended a friendly hand, who knows what may come of it.

Food for thought for the New Year.

TWENTY

"So, the old dump my father left me is being used by tramps. Sounds like a fine opportunity to try an experiment I have been anxious to implement. What matter if some wastrels are wasted...?" Seth grinned at his own pun.

The rental car and a disguise would guarantee Seth's ability to slip into town, set up the experiment and slip away unrecognized. Not that he actually expected that anyone in town would recognize the man who had once been the troubled boy who only rarely returned to the village with his mother to visit friends. No, that was hardly a worry and yet, it was such fun to pull this off incognito anyway.

Although he could avoid downtown in the village to go to the house, Seth decided to cruise through, just for fun. Like Scrooge, he scoffed at all the holiday decorations in every window and even on the historic old courthouse building where evergreen wreaths with red bows looked to him like a lot of foolishness.

The spiders sat in a box on the back seat. Lovely, talented spiders ready to move to the next level. Sure that he could feel their anticipation, he smiled imagining how the intruders would look when they were found. That would teach them.

It was not until late the next day when the same neighbor called the police station to say that he thought he smelled smoke coming from the Cobb house next door that the evil experiment came to light.

The dispatcher took the call and promised to send an officer around to check out the house. Jim was off-Cape attending a class in first aid and would not be back until very late. He planned to stop to visit his sister and her family in Westwood and drive home after that.

The new rookie cop, "Emery" Emerson was on duty and delighted to have something to do. When he took the job, preferring one in Boston or some city where they actually had crime, he figured he could move on later. Entering the house with the key kept at the station since the last problem there, he could not smell smoke. There did not seem to be anyone there either, no more people camping in the empty echoing house. However, somewhere upstairs he could hear something banging. Since he was there anyway, he figured he might as well check on things up there.

Heading for the stairs, he felt something bite him just up under the leg of his pants. "Damn, that hurts. House is probably full of bugs and mice and anything that can crawl or fly. Creepy place…"

Speaking aloud because it made him feel less creeped out, he suddenly felt lightheaded. Then, his stomach lurched and he vomited all over his shoes. He grabbed the railing, attempting to keep his balance but his legs suddenly turned to mush and he fell hard against the pine floor. Within seconds, the spiders went to work.

The next morning, Jim arrived at the station promptly at eight. "Good morning, Ellen, everything ship shape here?"

"Everything's good, Sir."

"Where's Emerson? Isn't he supposed to be here for the chief's meeting this morning?"

"He was called out last night and I haven't heard from him since. I guess he forgot to check back in and just went off his shift, Sir."

"Odd. Well, he will probably show up soon. I'll get a coffee and wait for him."

A half hour later, Jim checked with Ellen to see if Emerson called in sick, perhaps.

"No. I can't imagine him not doing so. He's been so punctual and good at the job since he started."

"Where did he go yesterday evening?"

"Let's see." Ellen checked the notes on a clipboard hanging on the side of her desk. "Oh, right, the house where some people broke in and were staying."

"The Cobb house?"

"Yes, that's it. A neighbor called worried that there might be a fire because he smelled smoke coming from next door. Emerson headed over there and that's the last I heard of him."

Jim raced out to his car. The sunny day had turned gray. Rain started to spit on the windshield as he drove fast to the old house. Ever since the bones were found in the bookshop and then the unbelievable spider webs appeared like dozens of yards of airy gray cloth that seemed to be trying to gobble up Libby's shop, Jim had not slept well. Not one to have nightmares, he had been plagued by them ever since then. Horrible scenes of monsters of every kind trying to kill him all night long. He woke in the morning exhausted from running away from these horrible creatures all night long.

Maybe he should have brought along backup. Well, he thought, when this turns out to be nothing and Emerson admits to meeting a gorgeous woman who wouldn't let him leave that morning, everything would slip back to normal.

Why couldn't he believe that, though?

Nothing obvious in the kitchen, Jim headed into the front hall. In the low light struggling to come in through the filthy windows, he saw what he assumed was a tightly rolled up rug at the foot of the stairs.

No, he thought, that was not there before. Better check upstairs; the campers might have returned.

Three hours later, Chief Walter Babbitt sat with the doctor he called when Officer Finlay came through the door looking as if he'd seen a host of ghosts. "Damn it, Jim, are you ill?"

"Chief…Oh, chief, I never saw anything so awful in my life. God, I was so terrified when I saw the hand. When I realized it was a human; not an old rug."

Finally, after the doctor provided a mild sedative, Jim was relaxing enough to tell the story without breaking down.

80

"The new officer has been so good at the job. When Ellen told me he hadn't reported in after being called to the old Cobb house to check on possible smoke I guess I didn't take it as odd, at first."

"Just take your time Jim. What happened?"

"Well, there was no sign of those people moving back in or anyone at all being there." Jim's breath is coming in gasps however he tries to hold himself together despite what he saw that shattered his nerves. "I could not find anything smoking. Couldn't even smell smoke. Of course, I thought I should check out the rest of the house, just in case."

The chief has never seen one of his officers so upset by a crime scene. "Just try to relax Jim." Easier said than done.

"Look, Jim" the chief added, "you can tell us later if you want to... maybe take a nap or something first."

"No, Chief, I need to tell it. I'm okay now, really. So, I headed for the stairs and I thought that what I saw on the floor at the bottom of the stairs was an old dirty rug rolled up. Nothing so unusual in an old house, except that it wasn't there the other day. Then...oh, God, then I saw fingers, a hand, well, part of a hand."

The next morning, the forensic department called to report on their attempts to extricate the body from the casing.

TWENTY-ONE

"Fingerprints are definitely those of Officer Emery. Although the body is still encased in something damned strange. Have no idea of what it is. Looks like a dirty old blanket or rug but we have been unable to remove it from the body. Got some guys here with powerful saws and they are totally frustrated. Seems to be some kind of super fabric." Kiddingly, the man suggested that it might have been aliens who did the killing. The Chief was not amused.

"Just keep trying. The officer was a young man, just out of the police academy. Nothing to kid about."

"Sorry, of course not. Will notify you when we have made some progress."

"That's crazy, Chief. What the hell could it be?"

"Don't ask me, not a hint. I guess they tried a very sharp saw and now they are calling in an expert on fiber. Meg at the lab says it looks like some kind of super plastic, but it is as tough as steel."

"Holy shit, feels like we slipped into some kind of horror story. Well, the hand that managed not to be covered at least provided us with identification. Poor fellow, his first month on the job and this…" Jim looked so pale the chief suggested he stop in to see Doc West. Jim answered that it was not necessary so the chief changed his tune and insisted. "Just do it, Jim, I need you to be in good shape. Who knows where this damned case might go yet. If poor Emery's hand had not been left exposed we'd never know what happened to him. As it is, this is looking like something beyond our imagining. Just do as I say and report back here early tomorrow. Stop at the doctor's office and then go home and get some rest."

"Okay, maybe I need something to help me sleep tonight. Damn, I just can't believe this."

At the bookshop three days later, Libby was hauling an awkward, torn and filthy box down the stairs when Ben arrived.

"Here, let me give you a hand, Libby."

"Found this in the back closet upstairs. I have been putting off going in there but when I was following an unpleasant smell it led me to the nasty closet. Full of books and some other stuff I do not look forward to inspecting."

"Maybe a treasure the old bastard hid with plans to sell it and move to Bali."

"Or, just more trash to deal with."

"How about here?" Ben put the box down on the table Libby had set up to use for just such work. On it were assorted paint brushes, glues, and a half full bottle of something Ben could not identify. Book cleaning and preserving stuff she had called it.

"I guess you heard about what happened at the empty Cobb house, Libby."

"Everyone in town has heard about it Ben. I was at the bakery this morning when three people were talking about it. Carrie told me that the chief wanted to keep it quiet until all the tests were done but instead it is flying around town like a rabid crow. Fortunately, all my customers for the past few days were from out of town so I didn't have to answer any questions."

"Did she tell the whole story?"

"Only that poor Jim Finlay found the body at the Cobb house and it has been identified as poor Officer Emerson Emery."

"It seems that two teenaged kids were hiding in the house when Jim got there and found the body. They evidently climbed in through a broken window in the rear of the house and when they heard Jim come in they hid behind a piece of furniture. When he went outside to call it in they snuck out and saw the body. Well, if a hand had not been sticking out of whatever it is that's wrapped around the body they would also have thought it was a dirty old rug. That's what Jim thought until he saw one hand, well, the fingers of one hand, sticking out." Ben cringed. "Not what one expects here, is it?"

"Well, the town is hysterical." Libby went to fill two cups with espresso.

Ben accepted the cup and sat across from Libby in the reading nook. "I stopped by the station and it is mayhem there. The story has morphed into a number of versions, of course. Some are saying that aliens murdered Emerson and wrapped him in some kind of alien, impenetrable cloth as a warning as to what they could do if this planet does not shape up soon."

"Well, this morning when I went out to get the mail from the box Maggie Webb stopped to share her version. According to her, my uncle has returned and he is out for revenge. Maggie is sure that when Emerson was a little boy he stole a book. She is making a list of everyone who ever had a run-in with my uncle so she can warn them. This is outrageous, Ben."

"I had a few words with Jim and he is in bad shape. He told me that he thought, after he saw the hand, that someone had rolled the body up in a rug hoping it would rot away and never be discovered. Of course, it would have been if it had not been for the hand, er, the fingers."

"But, Ben, let's apply a bit of logic here. Who would have had any reason to murder sweet Emerson? He could not have had an enemy in the world. He was such a sweet man."

"You got me. Just have to wait and see. Great espresso, by the way."

Two hours later, after a brisk sales day in the bookshop, Libby finally got to gingerly inspect the broken and tattered box awaiting her. Tired, not from waiting on customers but from listening to so many outrageous stories surrounding the death of Officer Emery, Libby could not wait to begin her inspection.

Even a box filled with mouse dirt, dead bugs, and possibly some rare allergy-laden dust long waiting for someone to breathe it in seemed a restful pursuit. Slipping on the protective suit, mask, and gloves Libby thought; *If only I were to find a book of extreme value, in the hundreds of thousands, what would I do?*

Deciding that she would continue doing what she was currently doing, despite a sudden windfall, she picked up the first filthy and broken book. Although, on second thought, she considered perhaps taking a bit of time to visit Rome, a place she had always wanted to see might be in order. Well, no time for dreaming. Here goes.

Hours later, the sun having sunk into the bay unnoticed by Libby, she found the bottom of the filthy box. On the way to the bottom, she found ten books. Four in very bad shape and six that might possibly be saved. What she had learned from her first bookshop boss, the lovely man from whom she bought the shop in Hastings, was that working with old books was akin to being a forensic archaeologist.

"They work with old bones and we with old books. Both grow brittle and stained with time. Care must be taken at every step to guarantee that nothing important is lost. Never rush your examination. Proceed slowly and cautiously if you wish to learn the history of an old book. It is not simply the date of the printing, the printer, the publisher or the quality of the cover that matters. No, each old book has a story to tell. Not just the story revealed on the pages but the story of where it has been, how it has been handled and why it lasted from then to now."

Libby had no idea of how long she had been working until her stomach growled. Standing and stretching felt good. Her neck was stiff and her legs felt weak from sitting far too long. This was always how it was when she became absorbed in inspecting old books.

Yet, she felt pleased. Smiling down at the books sitting on the table, dusted and cleaned, she reminded herself of the importance of this work. When she first went to work for Edgar Lowes in Hastings he insisted that she read Locard's book *Memories of a Criminologist* so that she would understand the "…crossover between our work and that of someone who solves crimes."

Years later, a book arrived in the shop after a writer of British crime novels died and his daughter cleaned out his house. Going through the fascinating collection of books the writer obviously depended upon to make his writing as professional and as knowledgeable as possible, Libby found *Locard's Exchange Principle.* Research told her that this book remains the backbone of forensic science collection and recovery to this day. She recalled her teacher and mentor's own words reading Locard's; "every contact leaves a trace".

Eleven p.m. No wonder I am famished and exhausted...albeit a satisfying version of exhausted. She had cleaned the books as much as she could to at least remove all traces of mouse dirt and the brown squiggly marks that are mouse pee. As always, when books are stored in among other things, there was an assortment of mouse nesting material from long ago stored clothing or furniture that evidently sharing the closet. Overriding it all was the smell of decaying paper that Libby knew so well.

When she took over the old bookshop in Hastings, long having loved the smell that spoke of old books, comfy old reading chairs and years of happy reading, she soon learned that the alluring smell is actually decay. "Perfume to the book seller and collector's olfactory sense."

Both hungry *and* tired, more obvious was the need for a shower. Time to wash away the scent of old books. As alluring as it might be to certain people, it was other things she preferred not to think about that needed scrubbing away. In the shower it suddenly occurred to her that when she had pulled the box out of the deep closet she thought she saw women's clothing and shoes way in the back. Only then did she remember seeing a huge dead spider lying just to the right of the box.

Since it was dead, she dismissed it as unimportant. Now, her mind's eye shot her a picture of the ugly creature. Had she seen some red markings on the body? She couldn't be sure, but having learned long ago to trust both her intuition and her instincts, particularly this kind of instantaneous recall-experience, she decided to check on spiders local to the Cape with red markings.

In the middle of the night, she dreamed that someone was calling her name. *Elizabeth Cobb Kavanagh, I know about you. You must go like the others. The itsy bitsy spider...bit the pretty lady.*

TWENTY-TWO

"This investors' meeting is vital to the future of the Cobb Webb, Seth. This is your big chance, our big chance to make a fortune. I am begging you to stay calm and not insult anyone, please! Just for a few hours behave like someone…normal. Hold onto your temper or you could ruin everything."

"For Christ's sake Jeremy, shut the fuck up. My work comes first and anyone who does not fully understand how magnificent it is deserves to be told that they are an ass. Just set up the display and make sure that I have everything I need to show them my genius invention."

The meeting room filled up just as a heavy rain began pounding on the roof. The Cobb Lab was situated in an old warehouse near the Boston wharfs. Seth was warned by a man he hired to do some interior work that the roof was in bad shape and needed immediate attention. Seth ignored him so water penetration had worked its way down many of the walls discoloring them and, on damp days, the stink of mold was sometimes overwhelming.

Seth did not mind therefore, he cared not that others found the place disgusting. His business partner Jeremy Collins, a college friend, had tried to convince Seth to move the meeting to a local hotel but Seth, as usual, denied the problem as calling for a change.

"The Cobb Web will alter the world as we know it. Soon, space will be penetrated by ships constructed of the Cobb Web. When the first black hole is entered by humans they will be travelling in a Cobb Web vehicle. Ships will sail the ocean impenetrable to anything the weather can throw at them. Cars will be safer than ever before because the Cobb Web will render them stronger than any moving vehicle has ever been, collision damage will no longer be an issue."

87

"What about sports gear? Mountain climbing and cave exploration, for instance?" This from a woman who owned one of the foremost clothing manufacturing plants in the country and was prepared to invest.

"A wasted query. It goes without saying fabrics manufactured using the Cobb Web will be superlative. Don't bother me with questions you can easily answer for yourself."

A voice from the rear of the room. "You mentioned in your report that you had carried out an important experiment with the Cobb Web. Please tell us about it."

"If I wanted to share the results I would have by now. That's it, no more questions. Meeting adjourned."

"There he goes again. I have never heard the man speak without infuriating everyone in the audience." This from a man who hoped to invest in the new company.

The man sitting next to him leaned closer, "Why doesn't he hire someone less obnoxious to present this information if he hopes to get investors?"

"Because he doesn't give a damn whether he is liked or hated. His arrogance, fortunately for him, cannot diminish the fact that the Cobb Web is sensational and will make investors very, very rich."

"So, you are going to go ahead, then?"

"Absolutely. Seth Cobb is an obnoxious asshole but his fabric is colossal. I would love to know about this latest experiment however, I have seen examples of what the fabric can do and that is enough for me to want to invest."

TWENTY-THREE

"What a great find, Libby. Maybe there are more hiding places yet to be discovered. I love the mystery."

Libby laughed. "Katy, believe me, you would not love the mess. Mouse dirt, dead bugs, decades of dust. Although, I must admit that the find yielded three very good books that one collector is very interested in."

"Was that all there was in the closet?"

"I don't know. The box was right in the front so I didn't dig any deeper. Although I think I saw some clothing and shoes further in."

"Oh, Libby, could I check it out, please. Maybe there are more books."

"I don't know Katy, old dust and bugs can be dangerous if you breathe them in. Your mother would never forgive me if you got sick from rummaging around in dirty old closets."

"I could wear one of your masks. And gloves. Oh, please, I would love to find a treasure. Hey, maybe the old coot hid a fortune in one of these still undiscovered places. This old house probably has all kinds of secret hiding places."

"Alright, but you will wear all the safety gear and do not stay in there too long."

"Good morning, Mrs. Wells, how nice to see you. What can I do for you today?"

"Well, as you know, my son Vincent collects old books about Cape Cod. I need a nice Christmas gift for him. What do you suggest, Libby?"

"Well, let's see what he has already." Libby pulled a ledger out from under the counter."

"Well, he does have a fine collection however I do believe I have just the thing. It came in last week. Simply called *Cape Cod Ways*. I think Vincent would love it."

One after another, customers filled the shop searching for gifts for others or themselves. Libby loved it when the reading nook was filled and everyone was enjoying the coffee and tea available. *Cozy* was the word that came to her mind, sure that no one would ever have called the shop that when her uncle ran it.

Libby was dusting the shelves when Katy slipped back into the shop. Libby turned to see that the girl was looking pale and disturbed. She went quickly to Katy who motioned for her to come away from the counter. They headed to the back away from the customers.

"Are you ill, Katy? Oh, I shouldn't have let you go into that filthy space. Did you keep the mask on and…"

"Libby, more bones."

"Jim, the body will not be any more dead if you wait until closing time. *Please*. It has been such a busy day and it is only a little over an hour until closing time. I would hate to upset my customers at holiday time."

"Okay, but I will be there right on the dot of five, Libby. Is Katy alright?"

"Yes, she is one tough lady. This is her second find but she is amazing. Carrying on working with customers as if nothing untoward has happened. I am in far worse shape than she is. See you at five."

When Katy returned to the counter for a Cobb's Hill Bookshop canvas bag for a customer she smiled at Libby. "These certainly are a hit. Pink book bags with such a lovely picture of the shop will be showing up under Christmas trees everywhere this year."

"Katy, why don't you go home early. I am fine holding down the fort."

"No thanks, Libby, this is helping me to deal with things. Hey, I am an old hand and finding bones now." She laughed and Libby had to join in. "I certainly chose the right person for not only the shop but the mysteries within."

"I have always loved mysteries, Libby. Never thought I'd get to live in one however."

Libby hugged Katy and went to speak to a man who needed help.

"So, you went to look in the closet for possibly more hidden books, Katy, right?" Officer Jim arrived right at five and now the four of them were sitting in the book nook. Libby called Carrie to tell her what happened and she had joined them when she closed the bakery.

"I did everything Libby made me do. I was wearing a mask and gloves and I moved things carefully. I found some ladies dresses and shoes and some blankets. The blankets were all a mess, looked like they were chewed on."

"Mice love to make nests out of wool," Libby added.

"So, I went deeper. I couldn't stand up in there, a very low ceiling. I found some kitchen stuff. Dishes in a carton and silverware in a wooden box. Very pretty, lined with tan velvet. Then, when I pulled that away there they were." Despite her seeming calm, Katy did a little shiver. Carrie reached out to take her daughter's hand.

"Thanks, Katy. You have been very brave…and helpful."

"What next, Jim?" Libby feared that the shop would have to be closed again at its busiest time of the year.

"Carrie, you can take Katy home now. Thanks for your help, Katy. Sorry you had to go through this." Jim smiled at Katy and thanked Carrie for coming.

"Libby, the Chief asked me to ask you if you have come across Grover's books. Business stuff, maybe sales ledgers or bank statements, that kind of thing."

"Well, there is a trunk upstairs that I haven't gotten around to checking. I did open it and have a peek inside. There could be that kind of thing in there."

"Great. We will need to check on everything that might give us a hint of what went on here over the years. Tell me again what the witch told you about a body."

"Oh, yes. Well, she took me down a dirt lane, very overgrown, hardly a lane anymore although it looked as if it had been at some time in the past. She pointed to a rock, medium size. She said that Grover buried someone there and rolled the rock on top. She said she saw him doing it. Something about there being a full moon and she always goes out to… How did she put it, oh, yes, renew her energy from the moon's ray. I think that was it."

"She may be a crazy lady, Libby, but sometimes she is spot on. I will have to talk to her."

"What next. At least tomorrow is Sunday and we are closed but please tell me that I will not have to close all next week. The week before Christmas."

"No, it will be fine. The crew is on the way to get the bones and then we wait for the forensic report. No need to close the shop. Just stay out of secret closets for a while, Libby."

"Have no fear, Jim."

"Buck up, Libby. One of these days this place will be mobbed with people fascinated with the stories about the place. Nothing like hauntings and such in these old Cape houses to bring in the crowds. In this case, paying crowds.

TWENTY-FOUR

"Chief, it looks like Grover Cobb murdered a bunch of women and hid their bodies in the shop and possibly buried some around town."

"Damn his nasty hide. Right under the town's noses, he was evidently taking in women and killing them. Probably the wacky bastard considered it a hobby. The man was a freak and a monster. I want you to take over Jim. You will need to find everything you can about Cobb's business and personal life."

"Yes, Chief. Libby says there is an old trunk that just might contain all that kind of stuff."

"Good, check it out today. Customers, book collectors, salesmen, cleaners, plumbers, electricians, anyone who ever stepped through the doors of the shop we need to know about. Anyone of them might know something. Of course, many of them will be gone, deceased."

"Well, there is always the grapevine. Things get around. Sometimes, it is only by starting to ask questions that it is possible to set off a tidal wave of information, as you know, being a small town."

"Start with the older people. Gently. Don't upset them, but see if anyone has any memories of strange women in the shop when they visited."

"I need to talk to Abby Dunne."

"Be careful there, Jim. You do not want to upset the dear lady unduly."

"Boss, Abby is just about one of the toughest women I know. Tough in that she does not get upset easily about anything. According to Libby, Abby was her mother's best friend and they shared everything. She probably knows more about Grover's women than anyone, even if second-hand."

"Okay Jim, but start with Grover's records, anything you can find. The man lived over the shop and it seems that everything pertinent to his life ought to still be there somewhere

93

on the premises. Identifying these women will not be easy or even very possible unless they have criminal records, of course."

Libby's curiosity got the better of her. Reassuring herself that everything strange and probably criminal that had transpired in the shop had done so years ago, she sat by the old sea trunk. Telling herself that she had cleared away all the negativity and replaced it with joy, hers and her customers', there was nothing to fear.

A handsome heavy wooden trunk that was once painted dark blue but was now faded and dull, the lid had instead been left unpainted and oiled. Libby grew up with old things. The old sea captain's house had been in the family since the days of whaling, since one family moved from Nantucket Island to settle in Barnstable when the sea captain turned from whaling to trading with Cuba for sugar and rum. Every piece of furniture had been there since then. Up in the attic were overflowing trunks of clothes worn by the families who lived there, as if any one of them might climb the stairs any minute to search for a favorite dress or parasol.

Libby looked down at the trunk imagining the trips it might have made aboard ship, in the captain's quarters. She touched the lid. But before opening it she could not keep herself from fearing that inside there might be yet another body. White bones bent to fit within.

Telling herself that she was now hardened to such things, although she felt a shiver race down her spine, Libby opened the trunk.

First, the familiar scent of rot, then the dead bugs but no immediate sign of mouse dirt. Feeling like a detective, Libby ascertained that the bugs would have flown in whenever Grover opened the trunk however mice would have no avenue for entering. So far, no bones, just what looked like ledgers, letters and notebooks. The treasure trove she was looking for. Jim would be delighted with this find. Now, perhaps they could begin to solve the mysteries.

Later, lying in bed unable to sleep, it occurred to Libby that if Grover was one to keep a diary everything just might be there, revealed in all its gruesome horror. Maybe, she might be inspired write a book about what occurred in the pink bookshop before she inherited it and restored it into a happy place.

That night, she dreamed about things she had only read about in books. She awoke more exhausted than when she laid her head down to sleep the previous night. Tea. She needed copious cups of tea.

TWENTY-FIVE

"**O**h dear, Jim, I have been straining my brain ever since I recalled Libby's mother's remark about seeing different women at the shop each holiday season when she deigned to visit her brother." Abby sat across from the Chief ringing the life out of a handkerchief. "I wish I could supply more information but that's about it. Oh, wait. I do recall back when Police Chief Williams was still here there was something…"

"Anything you can recall Abby would be helpful."

"Yes, it was winter and Charlie Robinson used to walk late at night no matter the weather. He said it was the reason he was still around at ninety-two. Claimed that the salt air was more intense at night and it cleaned away the bad stuff in the air during the day. He was passing the bookshop when he heard what he was sure was a woman's scream."

"Did he check on it?'

"No, as I recall he told the chief the following day however. The chief visited Grover and told him what Charlie heard but Grover insisted that it was his cat. Said the cat jumped onto the woodstove by mistake and burned its paws."

"And that was the end of it, Abby?"

"Well, I guess the chief figured that since Charlie was old maybe he heard wrong. I suppose a cat in distress could sound like a woman in distress."

"I suppose. Well, Abby you have been a big help. Please call the station if you remember anything else."

"Thanks so much for coming in Mrs. Winslow."

Winifred Winslow, the old woman everyone called the Witch of Barnstable sat primly across from the police chief. Wearing her usual black dress and a man's fedora hat she looked like something out of a children's book. Whenever he saw her around town he expected to see her suddenly lift off the ground and fly away. Or, simply vanish into smoke before his eyes.

"I hope you will be able to help us with an investigation Mrs. Winslow. You might have heard that there are some problems at the Cobb's Hill Bookshop."

"Don't beat around the bush with me. I remember you as a kid who was always in some kind of scrape. I suppose that's why you became a policeman, eh? I know what's going on at that place where Grover Cobb does his black magic."

Not often was he struck speechless. Searching for the right words that would not send this important witness running, he spoke gently, hoping to correct her without insulting her.

"Mrs. Winslow, you may recall that Grover died and his niece now owns the shop."

"Of course I know that. Lovely girl. Too young to run a business but that's how it is these days."

"You told Libby, Grover's niece, that he buried women, one woman in particular out behind the general store. She said that you took her walking out there, out near the swampy place."

"Yes. So what? Everyone knows that Grover is evil. All those women always comin' and goin' and him experimenting on them. But no one dares stop the man because he knows how to get even."

"Experimenting on women? What kind of experiments did he do on them, do you happen to know?"

"Oh, he thinks he is a genius. Grover the genius. He got those women to come here from all over the world. Told them he would make it so they never died. Ha! But they did die, didn't they?"

Then, as the words left her mouth, Winifred Winslow slipped into a deep sleep. Her mouth hung open and she snored loudly as the chief watched, dumbfounded.

He sat and waited, unsure what to do when suddenly she awakened as if she had not been asleep. "So, what I told Grover, a few weeks ago, was that I knew what he was doing and I wanted him to experiment on me so I would never die. I knew he wouldn't kill me if the experiment failed because I am a

Winslow. The Cobbs and the Winslows hate each other however, his son is part Winslow and that is important."

The chief thanked the witch and helped her up from the chair. His mind reeled from the insane interview. Nevertheless, it had revealed some important information. Now, all he had to do was separate the flotsam from the jetsam.

TWENTY-SIX

"Oh, Ben, you will not believe what I found in an old trunk."

"You look like someone who won the Lottery, Libby. Can't wait to hear about your find. I'd love a coffee if you have any made. Busy morning of divorces. Sometimes I wonder why marriage is still an option."

"Well, at least there is an escape route when a marriage goes bad. Lots of hot coffee. Have a seat."

Sipping their coffee the two sat companionably in the warm winter sun coming into the reading nook. The morning had been busy in the shop but now a lull felt good to Libby. Ever since she found the enlightening clues in the old trunk she had been looking forward to sharing them with Ben. She would have to contact Jim eventually, but first she needed to share with Ben.

More and more she depended on Ben for advice and loved their chats over coffee or dinner. Once a week, the two dined at the Dolphin or at the restaurant on Mattacheese Wharf. Not dates, or so she told herself, just two friends catching up.

Ben saw things differently. He had fallen in love with Libby the first time he met her when she came to his office to hear the will read. If she hadn't given off so many clues, insights into her seeming distrust of romance, by now he would have told her how he felt. Instead, he waited as she settled back into her hometown. He waited while she restored the old building so that she could live over the shop. He waited as she turned the business into a place people loved coming to even if just for the expresso and some quiet reading time. Now, he was tired of waiting. Every time he saw Libby he wanted to reach out and pull her to him. To kiss her until their hearts were joined forever.

"So, I have been putting off looking into this handsome old sea chest upstairs despite my curiosity. So much to do here before I could spare the time for digging through old trunks; despite how much I wanted to do so. I will never catch up if I get off my goals for this place. Curiosity not only killed the cat but it always interferes with being organized. However, I finally weakened. Guess two finds of human bones have loosened my self-control."

Ben laughed. "Libby, you amaze me by how calm you have remained."

"Funny how the bones have not affected me as I would have thought such a find would, I mean if I read about it in a book... Yet, they just seem to be peripheral to all the other things demanding my attention. I mean, naturally, the mystery is mind-boggling. However, somehow they just seem to fit into the character of my uncle. Oh, I am not saying this well. Let me begin again. It is just that old Grover was such a weirdo that even though I feel great compassion for the women he obviously murdered, it just seems to be part of the aura of this shop."

"The shop as it was. Not as it is now, Libby. Everyone who comes here is delighted. With your improvements, the new stock, the friendly reception, the tea and coffee etc. and with you, a far cry from grumpus Grover."

"That's so nice to hear, Ben."

"Anyway, it remains to be proved that Grover was a murderer."

"Oh, come on, Ben. What else could it be? Those two women crawled away and died. Of what, dust inhaling? Although, considering the way the place was that is not too far-fetched."

"If I may change the subject Libby, what do our dinners out mean to you? I mean are they dates or what?"

Silence. Libby's expression said it all. *Damn, big mistake, should not have asked. Damn, too late to retract the question.*

Then, she smiled and Ben's heart leapt as he waited for Libby to say something. Anything other than that she was so grateful for his friendship.

"Can we set that inquiry aside just for a few minutes, Ben? I am bursting to tell you what I found."

"Of course. That is why you summoned me, after all. What did you find?"

"The trunk is overflowing with stuff. Fortunately for the police, Grover's ledgers, everything related to the business seems to be in there. Looks like he kept good books despite his weirdo personality. However, what might just be of far more help to the police are the passports."

"Never knew he left the country, let alone the town, Libby. Why would he have had passports?"

"*He* didn't, but for some reason he collected the passports of a number of women."

"Crazy. What could that mean? Curiouser and curiouser."

"Well, the women were all from other countries. One from Poland, one from Scotland, another from Russia, etc. So, the question is, why would he have had access to these passports? Unless, of course, he murdered them all and kept their passports for souvenirs."

"Or, they worked for him. This might sound crazy but what if he did employ women who came here to start new lives. He could have been in contact with an agency that found work for people new in the country."

"Or, Grover could have murdered them and hid there here and there. Don't forget that the Witch took me to where she insists Grover buried a body."

"Have you told Jim?"

"Not yet, I wanted to tell you first."

Ben liked the sound of that.

TWENTY-SEVEN

"This is the lot. In an old sea trunk that evidently served as office files for my uncle." Libby laughed as she accepted a cup of tea from Jim.

"Well, the man was unorthodox so why not? File cabinets are for ordinary people. This is great. Just what the Chief hoped we could find. Thanks for doing the detective work for us."

"You know, Jim, I am thinking of writing a book about this whole crazy experience."

"Don't you find it kind of creepy living there where two sets of bones were found, Libby? Maybe you ought to find a nice house to rent. My cousin Maggie is in real estate."

"Thanks, Jim, but to paraphrase, like sticks and stones, bones can never hurt me. It is intriguing, not frightening. Any news on the latest bones?"

"Yup, got the report right here. Died about the same time period, give or take a few years. This report says that as close as they can come is that they probably died in this century. Well, not the twenty-first but the twentieth century. During Grover's time, eh? The up-date on the first set of bones that matches the latest set is that there is no evidence of injury, not that that tells us much. Could have been poison, I suppose."

Libby turned to look out the window of the office, sipping the tea and letting her mind wander as Jim answered a call. *Might be time to stock more mysteries set on Cape Cod. New writers. Surprised at how many books have been written recently that are set here.*

Turning back to Jim who was shuffling papers on his desk, Libby asked, "But why did he kill them, *if* he killed them? If it turns out that the murdered, sorry, dead women came from foreign countries then the agency that sent them to him ought to show up somewhere."

"Let's hope. I'll go through this stuff over and over until I have every bit of helpful information it can yield. Big help, Libby, thanks. The chief is in Boston but he is going to love this caché."

"Great. Take good care Jim. Might become very valuable treasure as the mystery evolves and avid mystery fans hear about our local excitement."

"Are you really sure you don't want to move out of the shop, Libby? Just until we find out what happened."

"Jim, what is there to be afraid of? Well, mice, bugs, dust and such but I am gaining on that front. Drop by and see how nice the place looks. Ta da!"

Libby had just sat down to eat her dinner when the phone rang. "Hello, Cobb's Hill Bookshop, Libby speaking." Nothing.

"Hello, who's there, please?" A noise like crinkly plastic wrap, as she later told Jim, but no one spoke.

Then, a voice that sounded to Libby like someone who has sand in his or her mouth was the only way she could describe the person who spoke the words from her nightmare.

"The itsy bitsy spider…killed the pretty girls."

When Jim arrived, just minutes later, Libby was trying valiantly to seem undisturbed and failing badly. "Jim, you will never believe me…" Shaking and feeling as if she were outside naked on a snowy night, her entire body so cold that her hands and feet ached, Libby told Jim about the strange call.

"Oh Libby, I was afraid of something like this. Did the caller say something else other than what you told me on the phone?" "No but I have heard those words before." Jim led her to a chair and offered to make a cup of tea but Libby refused.

"Jim, I swear I dreamed that conversation. Just a few nights ago. Well, those same words. The itsy bitsy spider killed the pretty lady.., no, it was the pretty girls."

"It's okay Libby. Everything is going to be alright. I talked to Carrie right after you called and she really wants you to come over there and spend the night with her and Katy. Please."

"You don't have to plead your case, Jim. Let me get a few things. I do need to get out of this crazy place. I never believed in ghosts, but damn it, this has me a bit shaken."

Two days later, the chief asked Libby if she could stop by the station. Staying at Carrie's had been a good idea. Libby and Katy kept the shop open every day and went home to dinner and pleasant evenings watching Brit Box detective series. Libby tried to convince herself that there was nothing surreal happening after dark at the shop, her home, but the phone call had touched a nerve that refused to settle down.

"Libby thanks so much for all the stuff you found. We have been able to find the address of an organization once based in Boston that found employment for foreigners; females only. They supplied hotel maids, cooks, and as it turns out, bookstore employees. It would seem that Grover did regular business with them for about ten years.

"Do you think these poor women are the skeletons found in the shop?"

"Too soon to say but in a day or two I will have a report that will tell me pretty much definitely if they were not from this country."

"Oh, how can that be determined?"

"Modern forensics are absolutely amazing, Libby. Honestly, I had no idea this was possible. However, I have recently been informed that the bones retain certain clues to the water and food eaten as a child. You see, there are differences, say in the kind of minerals in water and such that can pin down one's origins."

"Amazing.

"The agency is no longer in business so we can't get into this much further than that. We do know that he worked with them a number of times. My guess is that each one of the women soon discovered what a miserable man he was and they kept moving on."

"Makes sense. Will you let me know when you get that report?"

"Of course. In the meantime would you like me to have an officer check in with you now and then?"

"Well, I have been staying with Carrie and Katy but I really need to get back to my own place. They have been great but I am sure that the phone call was just some crank taking advantage of the situation. Not easy to keep secrets here, is it? Someone was just playing with my head. I will be fine Chief, but thanks for everything."

Next morning, Libby headed for the old Cobb's Hill Cemetery to do some research. She knew that the Cobb family plots were on one side of the graveyard and the Winslows on the opposite, as far away from each one as they could be.

"Good morning. What a lovely job you are doing on the grounds."

"Thanks, nice to be appreciated. Do you have family here?"

"Yes, my mother was a Cobb."

"Well, nice to meet you Miss. I am James Crocker and this here's my grandson Stephen. Say hello, Stephen."

"Hello, I did some trimming around the Cobb graves yesterday, Miss. I love reading the stones. I get a history lesson every time."

Libby smiled at the boy who looked young but was so well spoken and, in addition he enjoyed history, one of her favorite subjects.

"Yes, always something new to read here, I have found. Even when you think you have read them all one surprises you."

"I know. Don't you love the old words, Miss?"

"I do. Please, Mr. Crocker, Stephen, call me Libby. I am now Libby Kavanagh. My father owned a couple of businesses in town years ago. I grew up here."

"Ah, of course, little Libby. Your parents were lovely people, rest their souls."

TWENTY-EIGHT

"You know that you are welcome to stay as long as you want to…need to, Libby. We love having you."

"Thanks, Carrie, I know and I really appreciate all you have done for me. But I need to get home and get back to normal."

"Well, we are just a call away. I truly mean it, Libby, any time, day or night. Do not hesitate to call or come back here even in the middle of the night."

Carrie reached up to a hook on the kitchen wall where an assortment of keys hung beside some knitted winter hats. "Here is a key to the back door. Keep it with you, please. I mean it, Libby." She reached out to pull her new friend to her in an embrace.

"Okay, now you are going to have me crying. Thanks again. Katy, see you at the shop tomorrow morning. The new books I ordered will be coming in tomorrow. We need to shelve them as soon as they arrive so as not to lose any holiday shopping. Bye."

Libby sat in her car already missing her dear new friends but also anxious to return home. She called Ben and was told that he was in court. "Okay, Maria. Just have him give me a call. Let him know that I have moved back home. Thanks."

As she drove the half mile, Libby's mind wandered to the day she found the things in the upstairs closet tucked under the eaves. Had she been more curious at the time, she might have pulled out the clothes she saw that looked like they belonged to a woman. However, it was Katy who found the second skeleton hidden under the clothes and some badly chewed blankets.

What if her uncle brought in foreign women who would have been pleased to have found work in such a lovely environment? Then, very soon they saw him for who he really

106

was and they tried to quit? What if Grover was so wacky that he refused to accept this and he murdered them, one by one, then he hid some of them in the shop and buried some of them around town? Damn.

Entering the shop that felt cold because she always left the heat down there as low as she could without freezing the pipes, she told herself that the dead cannot harm the living.

Wanting to believe her words, Libby hummed a little tune from her childhood. Turning on the lights, turning up the heat, and starting the expresso machine, she worked at keeping her spirits and her courage up and yet... A picture flashed into her mind. A spider with a bit of red still showing on its body although it was obviously long dead. Spiders. Spider expert. Arachnology is the study of spiders. Seth Magus, son of Grover Cobb.

The day was so busy Libby did not have time to think beyond helping customers and ringing up sales. Katy managed to catalogue and shelve all the new books Libby had ordered, as well as help Libby with customers. Not a day went by that Libby was not thankful for hiring Katy.

After Libby closed the shop and ate a sandwich she had not gotten to at lunch time, she re-read the list of new books. A nice mix of fiction and non-fiction set on the Cape and a few set on Nantucket Island. Among them were *Murder at Bound Brook* by Rick Cochran, *The Forever Summer* by Jamie Brennan, *My Heart Belongs to Brewster* by Cynthia Gallant-Simpson as well as her cozy mysteries, some set on the Cape and some on Nantucket, and *The Old Cape Cod House* by Barbara Struna among others.

Tired but unable to settle until she did what had been tickling around in her brain all day, Libby turned the sign on the door from open to closed. At least the curious thought was there in the very few spare moments when she was not enjoying the customers and the sales. Now, she headed to the newly patched place on the wall in the rear of the shop. The place where the first skeleton was found.

Someone from forensics had come for the bones and obviously looked around to check if there were any clues however, she could not shift the thought. She needed to see for herself.

It was easy to remove the nails holding the piece of plywood in place, put there until Libby found the time to hire a plasterer.

As the dark hole appeared behind the patch, a shiver raced down her spine. However, she was not about to let ancient history frighten her. Well, ancient in so far as she would have been either not yet born or just a child when the foreign women began arriving. She wondered if the women her mother told her friend Abby about, women she said seemed to be on drugs or something, were kept as virtual prisoners by her uncle.

Damn, how she hated the man she had never met.

She went for a flashlight and when she returned she knelt down and crawled forward, just enough to allow her to enter the hole, head and shoulders only. Shining the light around, she saw nothing but a bit of dust. The man who removed the bones had done a good job. There had been nothing in there with the skeleton, no clothes, books or anything but the poor tragic victim of the man she now thought of as a brutal murderer.

Ready to back out, something caught her eye over to the right. Was it a bit of fluff a mouse had dropped on the way to build a nest? On close inspection what Libby saw caused her to back out as fast as she could and in the process she bumped her head and caught her arm on a nail sticking out of the wall. Gasping, she knew how the victims had died.

Three cups of tea later, Libby knew that she would not be able to sleep if she did not share this insight with someone.

"Hi, Ben, sorry to disturb you. I don't even know what time it is…I had a funny thing happen tonight."

"No problem. It's only just past seven. What's up?"

"Could you come over, Ben?"

"Of course. Have you had dinner?"

"Uh, no, I guess I haven't."

"Are you alright, Libby. How can you not know if you have eaten?"

"Well, I have had a lot of strong tea but no, no dinner."

"Give me about twenty minutes. I will get us a loaded pizza. Will you be alright until I get there?"

"Sure. Yes. I will be fine. Pizza sounds great. Thanks, Ben."

"Yum, smells great, Ben. Come on in. Tea, or I think there is some cranberry juice?"

"Where would you like to eat? Shall I take this to the kitchen or would you prefer to sit over in the reading nook?"

Libby acted as if she had been asked something difficult to answer. She looked at Ben and seemed to be looking through him. He put down the pizza and reached out to pull Libby into his arms. She did not resist.

"You are obviously not okay, Libby. What happened here?"

Libby clung to Ben, her head against his neck, and her arms tightly hanging on as if she feared slipping to the floor.

Before either of them fully registered what was happening, they were kissing. Because it felt so good, so reassuring to both of them, they continued doing so for a long time.

"Sit here, Love. You need food. I will not leave you alone. I am here to protect you, darling Libby."

Looking into Ben's eyes Libby realized that what just happened was what she had long wanted. However, she had worked so hard at making sure that it did not, she had missed out on the one thing that could make her life perfect. She arrived scarred and determined not to fall for another man. When Ben became her friend she told herself that that was all she wanted from him. So why was it, she now asked herself, that she often dreamed of making love to Ben? Damn, she had wasted so much time avoiding her true feelings when she could have been enjoying this amazing feeling all along.

"Now, when you have eaten and rested you can tell me what frightened you, you do not have to face it alone."

"I know. Thanks, Ben. Thanks for being you."

She reached out a hand for a piece of delicious pizza and smiled at Ben. "Are you sure, Ben? I mean, were you just being nice just now."

Ben laughed and touched her arm. "Libby, I have been in love with you since the day you sat in my office staring out at the rain, half listening to me read the will and half wandering somewhere. All I could think of was that I wanted to be with you wherever it was that your mind was travelling. I never wanted to rush you because it was obvious that you had reservations. I mean, I figured you had had a bad love experience."

"Ben, men do not figure out things like that." Libby laughed. "Men do not have such insight as that."

"Well, I know that I am a man and I know that I could sense that you were holding back because you had been hurt."

Libby leaned toward Ben with a look on her face that he knew he never wanted to change. If she would look at him like that for the rest of their lives he would be the happiest man alive.

"Attorney Benjamin West, I will never, ever let you go. You are one in a million. Will you promise never to leave me?"

Then, they both laughed and laughed and hugged and kissed and ate the huge loaded pizza, every crumb.

Ben did not hear what it was that Libby had figured out that had so frightened her until the next day.

The next day was Sunday so Ben and Libby slept in late. Thoughts of a murderer uncle, tragic girls who came to the new country with high hopes only to end up as part of a great mystery and killer spiders had somehow been shifted to the Scarlet O'Hara file marked, *I will think about that tomorrow.*

The day was sunny if chilly. Bundled up and warmed from the inside by the revelations of their mutual love, the two walked on the beach at Mattacheese hand in hand. They collected seashells and Libby insisted they take home three dried and brittle horseshoe crab shells, "Father, mother and baby sized. How sweet. Amazing how they shed their brittle shells and eventually inhabit one so very strong to protect them for their very long lives."

Ben carefully placed the tan colored horseshoe carapaces into the canvas bag Libby had insisted they take with

110

them. "I am incapable of walking the beach without collecting. One of these days I will find the time to create some kind of art from all the seashells I have at home in jars."

"A second career, love." Ben had never been so happy. Sure, he had been in love before but never with the absolute right woman for him. Well, he told himself, the best things in life are worth waiting for. "I have seen horseshoe crab shells set into shadow boxes. They certainly are fascinating. I recently read that their blood is proving to be valuable in scientific tests."

"Yes, I read a similar article. Certainly is a good time to be alive as medicine moves to recognize the value of healing herbs, even cannabis, and now this ancient creature is aiding in healing. Libby bent down to pick up three clam shells that were still intact. "Interesting how they have a hinge holding the two sides together. It is however a very fragile hinge. I might set up a display under glass of the various types of shells to be found locally. Children would like that."

"Given their origin, supposedly 450 million years ago, I read that horseshoe crabs are considered living fossils."

"Yes and I read that their name is a misnomer because they are not really crabs at all but are actually in the classification arthropods." Libby stopped as if she had hit a wall. Ben continued walking unaware of her until he looked back and saw that she again looked as if her mind was a million miles away. Only this time, he could see that there was fear there.

"What's wrong, Libby, you look frightened. Are you ill?"

"No, Ben. No, I just remembered what it was that I figured out that caused me to call you last evening."

"How about we head to the Barnstable Inn for lunch? I have a feeling that it is best if we are sitting down for this talk."

On the walk to the inn Libby worked at getting her thoughts organized. Ben remained quiet, holding Libby's hand, aware that she was in deep thought.

"Oh, this tomato bisque is wonderful. Full of fresh basil and garlic. Yum. Looking forward to the lobster mac and cheese. Never thought I would say those words. Growing up in lobster territory, although as kid one of my favorite meals was my grandmother's mac and cheese, the two food groups were as far away from one another as the Moon and Mars."

Ben smiled at Libby. "What? That's a loaded smile if I ever saw one, Mr. West."

"Just having thoughts I know you are not yet ready to entertain so let's get on to your fright the other night."

Libby told Ben about finding a spider in each place where bones were found. "I can tell by your expression that what I am saying sounds like damned flimsy evidence of anything, Ben. However, I believe that the poor women were bitten by poisonous spiders and that is how they died. No, let me rephrase that: I believe that my uncle killed them in a way that he was sure would never be discovered. If they remained hidden, as it turns out they did, until they were just bones, no one would know how they died. He probably knew just where to find poisonous spiders, black widows or such. The perfect crimes. Why he did it we may never know, however."

"I don't know Libby. Kind of slim evidence. I bet you can find old crusty, long-dead spiders everywhere in the building. What old house does not have them?"

"Alright, further thoughts on the subject. We know that my cousin Seth who changed his surname to Magus is an expert on spiders, aka arthropods. Perhaps his father was before him. Let's suppose that Seth learned about them from him. Only he took his talent in a positive direction. I have also read about spider venom uses in medical science, since we have already mentioned new discoveries for horseshoe crab blood and ancient healing herbs. Like father, like son."

Ben started to speak as the main dishes arrived. Libby recognized the waitress. "Thanks, Emily, looks absolutely delicious. Oh, by the way, I have that book you ordered. Stop by any time."

The two concentrated on eating while the meal was hot. As they sat waiting for coffee and *crème brûlée* (delighted to learn that this was the favorite dessert for each of them) they picked up where they left their conversation.

"Okay, I know that you have given this spider theory a lot of thought Libby however consider this...Seth never knew his father, never spoke to him until he came asking for help with college tuition. So, although it pains me to burst your bubble, it simply does not hold water...or venom."

"Aha. I am ready for that argument dear Ben. Genes."

"Pardon me."

"Such things can and definitely have happened. Talents passed along through the genes even between say twins who were separated at birth or sons who never knew their fathers. Case in point: I knew a wonderful chef in London who had never had the least interest in food until in his mid-twenties he suddenly decided to become a chef."

"But..." Ben smiled as Libby put her hand out to cover his mouth."

"Not yet, I have a bit more to support my argument. This chef grew up in a well to do home where there was a cook. He never set foot in the kitchen. When he turned thirty and he discovered an old framed family tree in the attic he learned that his grandfather had been a French chef."

"Hm. Interesting. So, you believe that Grover dabbled in a poisonous spider hobby and for evil reasons we will most likely never know about, he used spiders as murder weapons. Then, without ever spending time with his estranged father, Seth grew up to be a respected arachnologist."

"Exactly. That is why the police need to contact Seth Magus."

"Ben took Libby's hand. "Odd yes, but before we go running with this information to the police we must consider that the shop, the old house that has been there for well over a hundred years, is bound to have dead spiders. I mean, if you found dead mice would you have flashed to murder by mouse bite?"

Libby smiled. "The fine calculating mind of an attorney. I know, it is sounds crazy to your lawyer mind however, my instincts have rarely failed me. Maybe I will contact the spider man myself."

"Libby..."

Just then an old friend from school whom they both recognized stopped at the table.

"I'll be damned, Peter Coffin. I heard you were coming back to town to live. And, if my source was correct, you plan to reinstate the boat building business down by the yacht club. So great to see you."

"Same here. And it's the lovely Libby Cobb Kavanagh aka Bookworm."

Libby smiled and reached out her hand to Peter. "As I recall you were known for leaving dead things on Mrs. Kennedy'' desk."

They all laughed. "Ah, I had hoped that time would erase my bad rep. but coming home can be a dangerous thing."

"Join us, Peter. Let's catch up. Love to hear your plans for the old boat shop."

"Wish I could but I am meeting a prospective client."

"Another time then."

"Love to have you stop by the bookshop Peter to see the changes."

"I have heard such good things about what you have done there Libby. I will bring my wife and sons by for a look. Got to go. Great to see you two."

That night, Libby dreamed of spiders, black, hairy, many-legged beasts that were six feet tall and in hot pursuit as she raced along the beach reciting the rhyme she learned as a child.

The itsy-bitsy spider
Climbed up the water spout
Down came the rain
And washed the spider out
Out came the sun
And dried...

Libby awoke screaming.

TWENTY-NINE

"**J**im, are you free? Have something to show you." The chief called from his office.

Jim left his desk where he was stamping fishing licenses because the dispatcher/secretary was home with a bad cold. He was happy to help. Once, he told a good friend that he was lucky to do police work in a town like Barnstable where city crime rarely came along. Now, with bones being found in the old pink book store, he wondered what might come next. His friend said that a cold case was hardly a sign of things to come. Jim tried to believe that was true but his gut told him something else.

"Here I am Chief. Just trying to catch up on a few things."

"Take a seat, this news is enough to knock anyone off their feet."

"Sounds serious boss."

"Crime lab in Boston sent a report on Officer Emery's death. The thing that looked like an old rug turns out to be…hang on, let me get the exact wording they used. Okay, here it is. *The body was encased in a fabric that at first puzzled all the experts until someone on the staff recalled reading about such a fabric said to be stronger than steel. Unfortunately, their research failed to bring up anything about such an innovation. Then, a student at Harvard, son of one of the scientists, told her that he had heard that a scientist had claimed that he has solved some ancient mystery about the working of spiders. It seems that this man, whose name has yet to be revealed, was said to be doing experiments with this process but all that the young man could remember was that the scientist's aim was to create a fabric that could be used to build spaceships and maybe bridges.*

"What? Spiders? What does that mean?" Jim could hardly believe his ears. "How could spiders…?

"Hold on, you won't believe this. I just got off the phone with an old pal of mine, Ed Willette. He says he read an article in a science journal that explained about how miraculous it would be if

115

a super-strong fabric could be created as a solution to safer cars, planes and many other applications. The article explained that there is something called spiders' "post-spin" involved in making this possible. According to Ed, this is something that has mystified scientists for ages. It seems that spiders can do something miraculous that stretches the fiber that they normally create to make webs. Don't fully understand this myself but according to Ed spiders can do something to align the molecules and in this way they increase the fiber's tensile strength. You have heard of Kevlar, Jim, right?"

"Sure, great jackets are made of it. Mountain climbers and such wear the stuff."

"Well, it seems that this secretive scientist is about to become world famous and very rich because of this discovery. Space ships and all kinds of super strong things will eventually be made from this amazing fabric that is stronger than Kevlar and steel combined."

"So, somebody already knows how to make this super strong stuff and…shit, experimented with it on poor Emerson. But who and why?"

"Mary, what the hell is this note you left on my desk."

"Sir, my name is not Mary…"

"Shut up and just tell me what this means."

Sigh. "Someone called to ask you to get in touch at that number, Sir. He said he was interested in some new fabric you might know about. That is all he would say."

"That's all he said?"

"Yes, Sir. Oh, wait, he said that a professor at Harvard suggested that he call you."

Seth returned to his office, banging the door closed as hard as possible. Looking at the note he realized that it was a Barnstable phone number. "What the hell is this? There's not a soul in that foul town that I would ever want to speak to."

Tearing the paper, he tossed it into the trash and poured himself a double shot of whiskey. "God damn that Sedgewick, who does he think he is handing out my name like I am some lacky with nothing to do but share my secrets. Rot in hell whoever you are."

116

"Good day, Winifred, how nice of you to drop by."

Libby was busy getting mail orders ready to go out and the last person she really wanted to talk to was the witch. "Would you like a cup of coffee or tea?"

The old woman all dressed in black said not a word. Walking around the shop looking left and right as if inspecting for dust or maybe, as Libby thought, trying to feel the spirits of the long dead, she gave Libby the creeps.

"Is there a particular book you are interested in Winifred?"

The old woman stopped in the rear of the shop, facing the wall where the first bones had been found. She made a kind of low wailing sound that gradually increased in volume. Libby crossed her fingers hoping that no one entered the shop to see or hear this weirdness. All she needed was for a potential customer to think that she was like her nutty uncle and that she was conducting a séance with the old woman everyone laughed at for her witchy antics.

Libby slowly approached the witch. "Please tell me what this is all about Winifred. If I can help you out I will but I do not want you upsetting the customers."

"There are no customers here, Miss Cobb, just you and me and the spirit of those on the other side." Libby wondered if the woman was mistaking her for her mother by calling her Miss Cobb.

"True, well, about no customers, anyway. However, someone could come in at any time and this would make them uncomfortable. Please tell me what it is that you are doing here."

Silence. The witch ran her hands over the wall, as high as she could reach and to the left and right. Libby thought about calling Ben or Jim but decided that it would be best just to handle the old woman by herself.

"Winifred, you really need to tell me what you are doing here. I have much to do with the holiday coming. Books to send out for Christmas giving, and such."

Winifred turned to face Libby and put her finger to her lips. "Do you hear them, dear?"

"Hear them? Who do you mean?"

"The poor dead women. They are crying out for justice. He killed them. I know because his spirit came to me on the day he

117

died. I suspected him, oh yes, I always suspected him but only when he confessed to me was I positive about the murders. He loved spiders, don't you know. Trained them he told me once. I laughed but he insisted that he could train them to do his bidding. Foolish man. I warned him once when he was just a boy and he tried to frighten me with one of them. A big, hairy black one with a red vest. But I threw it in his face and he ran away."

Libby felt ill. How could this peculiar woman know all this unless it was true? Too much of what she claimed fit into the scenario of what had happened there since she came back to run the shop. She needed to share this with Ben and Jim and the Chief. But first, she had to get the witch out of the shop immediately.

Behind her the bell on the door tinkled and Libby panicked.

She took Winifred by the arm and led her toward the rear door. Thankfully, the man from the landscape shop down the street had recently cut away the brambles and vines that made using the back stairs nearly impossible. Opening the door she patted the witch on the back, "Thanks for all this, Winifred. Very enlightening. I will be in touch. Have a lovely day. Oh, and Happy Holidays.

Libby sighed with relief when the woman left without another word. Returning to the front of the shop she greeted a young couple who asked if they could just look around for a bit.

Working at composing herself, Libby morphed back into the charming store owner. "Oh please, look to your heart's content. If you have any questions, I will be at the desk. There is coffee and tea and pastry in the reading nook. Enjoy!"

The rest of the day went just fine, lots of sales and interesting conversations with book lovers. Finally, at five, ready to lock the front door Libby breathed in deeply the chilly but welcome salt air. Clouds raced across the sky, a mix of snowy white and smoky gray, a harbinger of a weather change. Libby's father taught her as a child how to read clouds. As she began to close the door, first turning the OPEN sign around to CLOSED something fell from above, nearly hitting her nose. Looking down, on the sidewalk, lying at her feet, she saw something she wanted to believe was a rusted leaf. Just one of the oak leaves that hung on all winter, going from summer green to autumn yellow and then, as winter set in, turned rust colored but still refusing to shed all of its leaves as had all the other deciduous trees.

She slammed the door shut, locked it and raced for the reading nook to make herself a strong espresso.

THIRTY

"Ben, it takes a lot to frighten me, but Winifred the Witch really got to me. She talked about things that could make her a serious witness in a court trial. I mean, she made a case for my uncle being the murderer of the women whose bones were found."

"Sweetie, so sorry you had to go through that. From what you told me she certainly either has an amazing imagination or…well, I hate to say it but, magical powers."

"Considering that I found what appeared to be black widow spiders in both locations, we have to consider, as crazy as it sounds, that Grover was a murderer."

"Well, I suppose we can take solace in the fact that this whole adventure is in regard to a cold case, er, cases. Thankfully, no one in danger in the present time."

"Right, unless we believe in ghosts. We need to tell the police, right?"

"Yes, I'll call Jim."

"Damn that witch. Sorry you had to go through that Libby."

"Thanks but in a way it is a relief. Now we know the real story."

"Sure, if we decide that she is credible." Jim rose to make coffee. "Who wants another cup?"

"Consider this," Libby nodded yes for a refill, "Winifred knew my uncle well, it seems. None of us ever knew the man. She may be a bit ditsy now but what she experienced in the past could still be valuable in the matter. Don't they say that as people grow older they can forget what happened yesterday but long ago memories are still vivid?"

"Good point, Libby." Ben took her hand.

120

"So, should I tell the Chief that the case is solved? Grover brought women here on the pretext of employment only to kill them by spider bites when he got sick of them or whatever."

"The evidence seems to point in that direction, Jim." Ben rose. "Have to get to court. Call me if you need anything, Libby. Please, if the witch shows up again summon me immediately."

"So you can thank her for solving the Cobb's Hill Bookshop murder mystery, Ben?"

Ben leaned down to kiss her cheek and Jim smiled. He had watched Ben with Libby and known months ago what was happening. He admired his friend for his patience that had obviously finally paid off. He was happy for them both.

"Call me too, Libby. And don't let the witch get to you. Did you two know that once she was a schoolteacher in Orleans? She lived here in town but travelled to Orleans every day. I spoke to someone who knew her back then and he said that she was an excellent teacher, admired by her students. After she retired she joined a group who, as old man Swift put it, 'hunted for ghosts in old buildings' and she gradually got very peculiar. Some kids started calling her the Witch of Barnstable and it stuck."

"Oh no, not again."

Libby entered the shop from her apartment upstairs to find that once again everything was encased in a covering of spider webs. She just wanted to sit on the stairs and weep.

How could such a thing happen? It would have taken millions of spiders all night long to create such a mess. Just not possible. Like a child who hopes that by closing her eyes the scary thing will disappear, Libby closed out the scene and breathed deeply.

Then, she heard something moving. Had she left a window open, she wondered? The sound, like a draft of air, grew closer. The next thing she knew, Libby was waking up feeling terrible. Her head hurt and she felt sick to her stomach. She rubbed her eyes and attempted to focus. Her vision was clouded, as if there was something in her eyes. Continuing to rub, she felt a sticky substance on her fingers.

Her vision cleared a bit, but still there was a film across them. She tried to sit up but her stomach roiled and she stopped trying. Turning her head to the right she saw the window in her bedroom. The sun was shining in. Then, something blocked the light. She squinted. A figure, tall and broad shouldered stood there, or was it just a shadow? The thing moved closer and leaned down very close to Libby's face. She could smell whiskey on his or her breath. When the person rubbed his cheek against hers, the scratchy whiskers proved it to be a male.

She tried to speak but only a squeak came out. "You are a nosy bitch. You should not have come here. You should have stayed in England, nosy bitch."

Libby considered closing her eyes and concentrating on continuing to sleep, perhaps to end the nightmare and find herself awake in her own comfy bed. Then, she remembered that she had already gotten up that morning. Showered, dressed and had her breakfast of pumpkin cranberry bread and coffee. She loved Carries' wonderful sweet breads. She tried to recall if she had spent that day in the shop and had returned to bed for a nap. After all, it was still daytime. She would not have taken a nap in the middle of a business day unless she had been stricken ill. That was it, mystery solved. She had been ill and she closed the shop early and crawled into bed. She probably took a couple of aspirins and somehow her memory of the day had disappeared.

"Just like I killed the other bitches, I will kill you. They were so easy to kill. Such fun watching them die, slowly, in pain, terrified. Ah, even better than the sex. Once they knew that they could never leave, once the fear of the outside, of strangers, took over, they dared not refuse the drugs. I told them that they were ill and the drugs would make them well again. The drugs made them my slaves. Then, I grew bored. Time for the spiders. My little pals, anxious to nibble on their soft white flesh."

A noise. Pounding. Feet on the stairs.

Here, I am here. Help me! Libby did not know if she shouted the words aloud or only in her head.

The man grunted. She saw him running. Confused, she thought she saw the witch in the doorway.

"Libby, my love, wake up. I am here, you are okay. Oh, Libby, do you hear me?"

More pounding on the stairs. Libby could only think about how she had meant to buy stair runners to quiet the old creaky stairs.

"I really must go on-line and fine stair runners. Lots of things to catch up with after the holidays."

"Is she alright?"

"Yes, some kind of drug I would say. Did you reach Doc West?"

"Yes, he's on his way."

"Libby, please hear me, it's Ben, Love."

An hour later, still groggy but fully awake, Libby related the story that she still wondered about having been a dream and not reality.

"The last thing I remember somewhat clearly is going downstairs and finding the shop once again draped with spider webs. I guess I dreamed that part. "

"Sorry to say," Ben held onto Libby's hand as if he was keeping her from slipping overboard into the icy water, "that part was real."

"Again? Who would do such a thing? How would anyone do it?"

"Sure is a mystery, Love."

Jim sat on the end of the bed looking pained. "Oh, Libby, I wish I could put all this craziness to rest and make you feel safe again. Can you describe the man you say was in the room threatening you?"

"Well, he needed a shave and he had been drinking whiskey."

Jim laughed, hoping to lighten the scene. "Well, that makes my job easier. I have to arrest fifty to sixty guys within a few miles of here."

Despite her shock and dismay, Libby laughed and so did Ben. "So glad to have you guys here. How did you know I was in trouble?"

Jim looked at Ben who shook his head and sighed.

"Sweetie, Winifred appeared in my office an hour ago and warned me that you were in danger."

Libby's eyes widened. Closing them quickly because they still hurt, she groaned. "You mean that if it was not for the witch I might be dead and my body left somewhere to be found in a couple of decades?"

Doc West entered with his ancient black leather bag that Libby remembered from when she was a kid. He had taken over for his father, the former town doctor and he told her that using his father's old medical bag helped to make him a better doctor.

"Dear, dear Libby, what have we here?"

Rubbing her eyes with a cool cloth that smelled like a pine woods, the doctor made little sounds. "Oh, my goodness, so sticky. No wonder your eyes are red and sore, dear girl. Looks to me like spiders' webs. Did you walk into one, Libby?"

"Not exactly sure, Doc. Might have. Heaven knows my life has been riddled by spiders of late."

Ben took the salve and was told to have Libby apply it hourly to her eyes and not to go out in direct sunlight for at least a day. Jim excused himself promising to return with the equipment to take fingerprints in the room. "Try not touch anything, particularly the window sill. I believe he came in that way. That old, tough trumpet vine outside would make it easy to climb in. Remember to always lock your windows, Libby?"

"So now I have to sleep without fresh air, expect to find the shop encased in cobwebs each time I head to the shop, and live in fear of deadly spider bites *and* ghosts."

"That was no ghost Libby. I am moving in here to protect you."

"Hm, nice idea. Just what I wanted for Christmas, Ben."

.

THIRTY-ONE

"This is just too damned crazy. Can't be for real. Don't care if they are experts. Even experts sometimes get it wrong." Libby sat across from the Police Chief feeling anxious.

"Libby, fingerprints do not lie. I mean, we do not know yet who the intruder was because, of course, fingerprints are only traceable if the person has a record. However, they are new, clear prints. Someone climbed up the vine outside the window and tried to kill you."

In the interim between the terrifying experience and this morning when she was asked to come to the station to tell her story to the Chief, Libby had convinced herself that the entire episode had been a bad dream. She had no explanation of how and why she found herself in bed when the last thing she recalled was heading down to the shop to open after she had her breakfast. Okay, so the webs covering everything...*once again*, had been real, but she refused to believe that a real person entered her room and tried to kill her. If she believed that she would go running back to Hastings. She did not want to do that however. She loved her knew life. She loved the shop and reuniting with her old friends and she loved Ben with all her heart.

"Let's consider that it was food poisoning. Oh, no, Carrie's wonderful pumpkin cranberry bread could not be the culprit. So, it was something else something like asbestos or lead paint."

Jim entered the office in time to hear Libby's take on her experience. "Libby, we would all love to think that is what happened, but take my word for it, someone was in the room with you."

"Damn, damn, why?"

"That's what I am going to find out if it is the last thing I ever do." Jim stamped his foot.

THIRTY-TWO

Libby needed air. Maybe, she thought, if she went for a long walk and took in copious amounts of fresh salt air she would be able to clear her head of the craziest experience of her life.

She had never believed in ghosts. Not even living in a small Cape Cod town where every other house once belonged to a sea captain and everyone had a story about ghosts inhabiting these old mansions did she fall prey. She considered herself a rational person and yet this recent experience had been powerful enough to cause her to reconsider the possibility of ghosts. So far, however, no living person had become a suspect and she could hardly accuse Grover of some of the antics at the shop. Certainly his ghost could not have created the mess in the shop with webs that suddenly appeared to cover every inch of the place like a sticky gray fog.

The first time the shop filled with gauzy gray spiders' webs the expert who visited was astonished and yet, he had a theory about how they had come to tangle themselves throughout the bookshop. "This, shall we call it, *tangled book web* (the little man laughed although those gathered to hear his report, Jim, Ben, the Chief and she did not join him) could have a proper explanation."

He continued. There is one variety of spider that is only found in the Sahara and in some deserts in South America that is capable of creating large masses of web."

Jim interrupted the odd little man whose eyes never looked at his audience, instead, he seemed to be forever searching the room for something and now and then he shuddered. "So, someone who knows spiders and has access to these critters from across the world would have to have come here and planted them on purpose."

"Yes, Officer. Oh, most definitely. Ah, they are lovely, aren't they?"

126

The Chief asked, "So, where are these clever spiders now, Sir?"

"Well, you see, after they perform this amazing task, they die. They are so productive that they use up every bit of the necessary liquid and so they die."

"Liquid? Please explain what you mean by this, Mr. Gannett." Ben was obviously growing tired waiting for the man to supply a rational explanation for the mess in Libby's shop. He had had enough mystery and just wanted Libby to be safe from anymore danger.

"Well, you see, spiders, the magnificent little creatures, are silk producing factories. Inside their bodies, thread is stored as a highly concentrated liquid. Ah, in order to fully appreciate these magnificent creatures one must be aware that spider silk is a protein. As such, because proteins are formed inside of living cells, spider silk transforms from liquid protein to solid thread when it leaves the body. As opposed to the manufacture of steel which requires a furnace, the process of creating silk happens at body temperature. Human engineering is adept at using more and more energy to solve problems while our talented friends the spiders perform their engineering through the use of better information from Nature. You have got to love these creatures."

Now, walking along the beach, Libby recalled the funny little man's speech. She had been impressed by the information however, it went nowhere near figuring out who had brought the spiders from the Sahara or South America to her shop and why.

Was it a bookshop competitor, an unhappy customer, or maybe a witch having fun with her? No, on the last. Winifred might be odd and think of herself as being capable of magical powers, but she was just an old lady looking for attention. At least the spider expert convinced them all that these talented spiders had not found their way into the shop from the outdoors, a local bunch never before seen, maybe long slumbering on Cape Cod. Someone had to know of their existence, had access to them, and purposely slipped them into the shop to do their worst. Someone must want her to fail, to ruin her business by scaring the hell out of her and sending her packing. But who?

Libby had heard of runners getting a second wind but had never experienced that feeling. Today, she felt it, at last. She walked and walked on the beach and then, without consciously making the decision, she found herself headed for Cobb's Hill Cemetery not wanting to stop walking despite the chill air. Maybe if she visited Grover's grave...Well, she had no answer to what she might learn if she did however she felt the need anyway. As Libby headed for the west side of the well-kept cemetery where she knew the Cobb plot sat on a bit of rise backed by the Rosa rugosa bushes her mother had planted years ago she saw an elderly man and a boy working at trimming a large bush. "Everything looks so well kept. Are you responsible for the excellent upkeep, Sir?"

"Ah, good morning. Yes, my grandson and I volunteer as a town service. Always loved this old place; began reading the stones as a boy. Lot to be learned from doing so, don't you know?"

Libby reached out her hand to the man. "I am Libby Kavanagh, of the Cobb family. My family is all over there."

"Ah, the Cobbs. Know them all well. So, you must be Silky's daughter." Seeing her confusion, the old man said, "Oh, sorry, that's what some of us called her because of her pretty silky hair. Just like yours. A chip off the old block, as they say."

Libby laughed. She had never heard anyone call her mother that nickname.

"Oh, this is my grandson Stephen. Best helper I ever had."

"Hello Miss. You are the nice lady at the bookshop, aren't you?"

"Yes. Oh, I have seen you in the shop. Came in with your mother looking for something special for...oops."

"It's okay. Mom gave the book to Gramps early because she can never wait. She had been looking for that book for a long time. She couldn't wait until Christmas." They laughed and chatted some more.

"Well, just thought I'd visit my Uncle Grover's grave since I did not come to his funeral and he did leave me his bookshop. Perhaps it is time to thank him."

The old man looked troubled. Libby stood and waited, expecting him to say something about the man being a mean old bastard or that Grover had cheated him or something worse.

Instead, what he said shook her as if the earth had moved under her feet.

THIRTY-THREE

"I have completely revised my opinion on the ghost question, Ben."

She had told him about the caretaker at the Cobb's Hill Cemetery and he gasped as she had when the old man told her his experiences with her uncle. Post-mortem.

"He is a lovely man and his grandson is as well. The boy surprised me with his knowledge of history. He reads and loves the subject. At his age, well, when teenage boys are usually more interested in girls that reading, Stephen reads history and is very knowledgeable."

"So, the old man told you that he has had strange experiences at the gravesite since Grover was buried there?"

"Yes. He does not seem to be a fanciful man but he claims, and I believe him, that he has seen peculiar lights on the ground and seemingly hanging over the gravesite at night. Only on Grover's grave. He explained that he likes to walk in the cemetery at night when he cannot sleep. Kiddingly, he said, '*You cannot ask for better companions than the dead. They do not indulge in idle chatter. They do not play music too loud nor do they nose around in your business.*' He also said that he hears moaning and cursing, yes, cursing, from the grave. Maybe you or Jim should talk to him."

"Libby, I believe you. Although, I don't know what to say. Damn, please move in with me until this thing is straightened out."

"Oh, Ben, think about it, the old man said that someone had dug up my uncle's grave purposely. When he cautioned me that the grave had been, in his words, 'dug up and disturbed' I immediately thought he meant that an animal had dug in the earth. Then, he led me over to Grover's plot and anyone could see that a shovel had done the damage. Someone had dug up the earth although they had not dug deep enough to uncover the coffin. The old man said that he figured it was someone who had long carried a grudge against Grover and just wanted to exorcise the bad feeling."

130

"It does seem to be too damned coincidental. Maybe you should close the shop, move over to my place, and let the police solve this once and for all."

"No. Damn it, I am not going to let some nut drive me away. Problem is; what defense does one have against a ghost?"

They laughed and Ben hugged Libby although he had no answer to that most peculiar question.

"I took a look at the gravesite, Libby. What the hell happened there is anybody's guess. At least the body was not disturbed. Maybe it was someone he cheated or insulted and messing up the site was enough to satisfy him." Jim wanted to put Libby's mind at ease and yet he had some questions he needed to find answers to before he put the case to rest.

"Jim, things have gotten just too damned crazy. I will be moving in with Ben. Katy has been terrific about still working here. Although I will not allow her to be in the shop alone. By the way I found someone who would like to sell that book you are were interested in for your father for Christmas. Signed first edition. It is in excellent shape. Stop by anytime to pick it up."

"Great, Dad will be so pleased. I will feel much better with you not sleeping there. About your ghost…he was real. Well, not a real ghost but a real person. Not only fingerprints but soil found on the floor under the window. Soil from the garden below. Someone climbed up, for whatever inexplicable reason. Unfortunately, he has no record so we cannot identify him. Wish we could."

"What puzzles me is why this intruder would have a grudge against me. My uncle had enemies but as far as I know I have not made any enemies here. My customers have become friends and childhood friends have become happy customers."

"I will get to the bottom of this mystery, Libby, or turn in my badge."

Jim rose to walk Libby to the door where she reached out to hug him. Jim hugged her back and repeated his solemn promise.

"Good morning, may I help you to find something?" The woman looked to be in her seventies. She smiled shyly but said nothing. Libby stood behind the counter wrapping books for

131

shipment. If they went out that day they would arrive before Christmas according to the post office.

The woman approached the desk and Libby waited for her to speak. Finally, Libby said, "Have you visited us before?"

"I… Well, I have been here. Long ago."

A flash of alarm shot through Libby. As if she knew what was coming she braced herself for the worst.

"Do you mean when my uncle Grover Cobb owned the shop?"

"Yes. I knew the man. He was cruel, I hated him."

Tears fell from the woman's eyes and she began to crumble into her oversized coat. Libby hurried to put her arm through the woman's and led her to the book nook. Thankfully, it was lunchtime and the shop was empty. Katy had gone to pick up sandwiches so perhaps this was an amazing opportunity for some history.

Libby waited as the woman composed herself. She brought a cup of hot tea and held it out to the woman. "Thank you. I am so sorry. I did not mean to do this."

"My dear lady. Please know that I am fully aware of what a heinous person my uncle was. There is not one iota of family affection for him. I know all about him. You may trust me implicitly."

"Thank you. You see, I came here as a young innocent woman looking for work. I was born in Lithuania. We were very poor. When my parents died and I had no other family a woman from the organization that helped me with food and the occasional job, although I had no training to do anything, suggested it."

"It? Do you mean suggested that you come to this country and would be guaranteed employment and housing?"

"You have heard of this, dear?"

"Yes, it seems that my uncle employed a number of young women like you, looking for a better life."

"I know."

Again, the woman began to cry. She cried so hard she could not speak. Libby held her hand and waited, her heart aching for the poor lady.

Finally, the woman calmed down and drank two cups of tea. "Where are you staying Vera?"

"I have a room in the town called Dennis. A very nice house that has rooms to rent."

"Why did you return here…I mean if you had bad memories?"

"I read about Grover's death. I was happy to read. I am sorry if you think that is a bad thing. He was a very bad man and I am happy he is gone."

"No one liked him, Vera. I understand."

Vera stayed and talked for over two hours. When a customer came into the shop Libby waited on them and Vera waited, seeming to be content sitting in the cozy book nook. When Libby returned to sit with her just before closing time Vera said something that shocked Libby but also brought her to a decision.

"Oh, Ben, it was so sad. She told me so many things that are so horrible…almost unbelievable. My uncle was a monster."

"Darling, was what she told you helpful in any way?"

"Yes. Actually, very helpful, but confusing, as well."

For the next hour, the two discussed the woman's revelations.

Libby and Ben sat in the Chief's office waiting for Jim to return from court. Surprisingly, the talk was of books.

"So, you have read all of Nathaniel Philbrick's books."

"Yup. I loved every one of them. The man knows Nantucket Island and knows his history. Met him once at a book signing. My wife and I were staying at the Jared Coffin House for a bit of a getaway and he was doing a signing at the bookstore there. Real nice fella." Neither Libby nor Ben had ever heard the Chief be so voluble about anything beyond police work.

"Yes, he is. When he and his wife were in England a few years back I met them."

Libby and the Chief were deep into a discussion of two other writers of Cape Cod and the Island's history when Jim arrived.

"Sorry to be late, folks." Turning to Libby, "So you met a woman who worked for your uncle. A woman who came over from Europe."

133

"From Lithuania. She was so sweet, but still so shattered. What she told me was beyond belief. It seems that she was one of the young women who came early in the program. She was meant to work at the shop and she was even promised a room upstairs until she could find a place to live. All the arrangements were made and she was so excited about being in this country. My uncle greeted her as if he was delighted to have her and told her that it would take a while to train her. In the meantime, she would not be allowed in the shop during open hours until after the training. Naturally, she suspected nothing untoward.

Very soon, the sexual assaults began. The woman, her name is Vera, was locked in a room all day long and he came to her at night. She never was allowed to come down to the shop although some days when the weather was good he tied her to a kind of leash and let her sit on the top of the back stairs just outside the room to get the air. He gagged her so that she could not call for help. She said that at the time the vines made the back stairs impassable and as there are no other buildings in sight she knew that no one would pass and see her there."

"This is awful. No one knew what was going on there. Damn, damn. He was more of a monster than we expected." Jim shook his head and the Chief swore under his breath.

"Here is the part I think you will be most interested in, although it is all so terrible. It seems that one day a young boy entered the room where she was held prisoner. She has no idea of where he came from but she said he was a polite and handsome boy. She thought he was probably about ten years old. He was carrying a jar with him and he showed her what he had inside the jar. She recalls her horror when she saw the two large hairy spiders. However, the boy told her not to be afraid. He said the creatures were his friends. His *only friends*, was how he put it."

Jim stood and looked down at Libby. "Did he threaten her with the spiders, Libby, did she say."

"Well, no, he simply told her all about the spiders. Said they were called Wolf Spiders. Still, Vera recoiled at the sight of them. The boy laughed and told her that she was in no more danger from a wolf spider bite than from a bee sting. His words were, 'Wolf spiders produce a non-deadly venom that is designed to

134

paralyze their prey. The spider's venom is not especially toxic to human beings.' And she relaxed, she said."

"So, did this boy visit again?"

"Yes, after that day he came twice more, never however discovered by Grover who remained in the shop all day until at least seven o'clock. This is where it gets very odd." Libby caught her breath and Ben asked if she would like to finish the story at another time. "No. I need to finish now. Thanks but I really need to do this. So, each time the boy came he brought the same spiders and on the third visit he convinced her to touch them. Again, warning her that they would not hurt her. He told her that he had retracted their venom so that they could not do her any harm. Not even a bee-like sting."

"Just let me ask, Libby, did he ever say who he was?"

"No. She said he only said that he had come to share his friends with her because he knew that she had no one in this country. On his last visit, he brought different spiders for her to see. These were hairy, black, ugly creatures, according to Vera, and they had red 'vests' as she put it. On that occasion, he untied her hands so that she could touch the spiders. Then, he offered to untie her feet so she could walk around the room, telling her that she needed to exercise. There was a loud noise from downstairs and the boy dropped the spider jar and ran. To Vera's horror, although she had very gingerly touched one of the spiders to please the nice boy and it had not hurt her, when he ran and the spiders got loose, one of them bit her ankle. She said the pain was horrible. Of course, the boy had untied her and once she realized that she could run she did. She headed in the direction the boy had taken and found a doorway onto the side lawn. She ran and ran until someone on the street saw her and she begged the man to get her to a doctor."

"So, who was the town doc back then? He is our best hope." Jim rubbed his hands together, looking very pleased.

"Well, here is the rub, as Shakespeare would say, the man was from down-Cape and so he took her to his doctor. She never learned the name of the town but she said they drove for quite a long time and she was in such pain she did not pay much attention. The doctor saved her life and found her work in Boston. He even

135

hired someone to drive her there and that was the last time that she was on the Cape."

"Hell of a story. Who could the boy have been and how would he have known that she was Grover's prisoner?" The Chief now rose and headed for the coffee machine.

Libby was exhausted from telling her story so she and Ben headed to his place. All she wanted to do was sleep until she could decide what to do.

She had kept back one important piece information; even from Ben. Telling herself that she read far too many mysteries, still she was determined to put her suspicion to the test. What could happen? Maybe, she would find the truth and the craziness would stop.

Thus, Libby's plan began to take on a practical form.

Lying in bed, Jim also came to a very likely solution that he needed to follow up on. No way did he entertain the idea of Grover's ghost although he cringed thinking about the moment he had walked into Libby's shop and seen the…what did the weird little spider expert call it? Then he remembered the man's words; A tangled book web.

THIRTY-FOUR

The drive to Boston was very pleasant. The weather was typical of the week before Christmas on Cape Cod. Gray, chilly, and unsettled. Although the weather forecast did not predict snow, the sky looked as if it was simply holding back its onslaught temporarily.

Libby hadn't left the Cape for months. Every minute had been called for by the new shop restoration and building the business anew. Then, there was falling in love with Ben. As Libby drove over the Sagamore Bridge over the Cape Cod Canal she had a tinge of second thoughts. *No, I am in danger doing it this way. This is my mystery, my family. I need to do this and then share it with the authorities.* Knowing that Ben would have tried to stop her, she kept it from him. She would need to apologize and explain when she returned. The last thing she wanted to do was jeopardize their lovely new relationship.

Moving in with him, into his charming house, left to him by his aunt, with a magnificent view of Sandy Neck, had been the right thing to do. She wondered what would have happened if there had been no mysteries to complicate her life as a returned Barnstable native. It had been a wild ride, she had to admit. Thankfully, she had hired Katy who seemed not to be overly upset but rather intrigued by all the crazy things that had happened at the shop. It was both Katy and Ben who had bolstered her courage in dealing with things that might be classified as *things that go bump in the night.*

Now, she was headed to meet her only living relative.

THIRTY-FIVE

Jim and Ben met when each of them were at the courthouse on business. "Ben, I was going to call you. Got a few minutes for a coffee?"

"Sure. What's up?"

"It's about the stuff going down at Libby's shop."

Sitting at a table in the rear of the coffee shop, Jim shared his idea with Ben thankful that there was no one near enough to hear what he was thinking…and planning.

"I'm sure you have been thinking what I have been thinking about what has to be done next."

"Well, if it is about speaking to Grover's son Seth then I believe it is about time. Over time, possibly."

"Exactly. I have called his office a few times asking him to call the station but not a word from him to date. I think it is time for a visit. I plan to head to Boston in the next few days to interview him. Because he was estranged from his father he may know nothing but I have to be sure of that. Every avenue must be checked before we can put this mess to rest. I wanted to talk to you before Libby however."

"Don't mistake Libby for a damsel in distress, Jim. She is an amazingly strong woman and she would not be happy if she finds out that you are trying to keep this from her."

"I know she is, Ben. She has been great through all this but I just thought, well, okay, I will talk to her today."

"Tomorrow. Today she is off to meet with a collector off-Cape who has some signed books that could be very valuable. As I recall, there are some Kurt Vonneguts and some Norman Mailers. She expects to be home around dinnertime."

"Great. So, have you been thinking that the kid who visited Vera, the kid who collected spiders, had to be Seth?"

"Well, I have but then I wondered how he could have gotten there since his mother moved them to Bourne when she took a teaching job."

"Sure, too young to drive but there would have been other ways."

"Sure, I considered that but still there is the question of what would have motivated the boy to go to his father's shop if the man had refused to accept his parentage? Actually, they had never met until years later. As far as I know, they never even met until Seth came begging for help with college tuition. Pieces of the puzzle seem not to fit well enough to be sure that it was Seth who visited the poor trapped woman."

"True, but on the other hand, isn't it just too much of a coincidence that the kid was a lover of spiders as was Seth Cobb, er, Magus?"

"You have a strong point there Jim, what does the Chief say about it?"

"He wants me to question him as soon as possible. He believes that the kid probably wanted to get to know his father and found a way to get himself down there once in a while. Maybe the boy came into the bookshop and hung around unrecognized to spy on his father and get up the courage to speak to him. Not an altogether unreasonable conclusion I'd say."

"No, I like it. Yes, that makes a lot of sense."

"Chief thinks that at some point Seth discovered the unlocked door on the side of the house and snuck in. On this particular day he found the poor woman tied up, a prisoner, and although he would probably not have begun to understand why that was, it seemed like an adventure to him. She was a nice woman and he shared his love of spiders with her and, ultimately, by chance, he allowed her to escape."

"May I share this with Libby this evening?"

"Absolutely. Gotta run. Thanks for the time, Ben. See ya soon."

Libby entered Seth's office just as the secretary was preparing to go to lunch. "I am here to see Dr. Magus although I do not have an appointment."

"Oh, I am terribly sorry but no one sees him without an appointment. I could schedule you for some time next week."

"Well, perhaps I should say that he is my cousin."

"Oh, nice. Well, I mean nice to know he has some relatives. I mean, well, I didn't know that he did because no one ever visits him. No one but other scientists."

"Perhaps you might let him know that Libby, Elizabeth Cobb Kavanagh is here to see him."

Libby wondered why the young woman seemed so nervous. "Sir, there is someone here to see you…"

Libby could hear Seth's loud response. "You know the rules. Send her away."

Libby took the phone from the young woman who looked as if she had stuck her finger in a light socket.

"Seth, I am your cousin. I have come all the way from Cape Cod to meet you and unless you are in the middle of life-threatening surgery I would appreciate a few minutes of your time."

The two women stood there, one of them visibly shaking and the other annoyed enough to consider simply walking into the office.

Finally, Seth appeared in the doorway. Libby was surprised to see how good looking he was.

"So, you are a Cobb. A Cobb snob is what everyone called those miserable people who messed up my life."

Libby nearly laughed. She felt as if she was being addressed by a young boy, not a grown professional man, a respected scientist.

"Well, I am not a snob however; I do practice good manners, something you obviously missed in your upbringing." Libby, never having been one to tolerate fools gladly turned to leave.

"Wait!"

Libby stopped and turned back. "You, Mary or whatever your name is, get out. Take a long lunch break. Go, scoot."

After the girl left Libby waited although not foolish enough to expect an apology.

"I can give you two minutes."

Torn between leaving in a huff and satisfying her curiosity, Libby walked slowly into Seth's office. Hit by the smell of something odious, she looked around the room, noting that it was as cold and impersonal as a morgue.

Seth sat behind his desk grimacing. Libby took the seat on the opposite side and smiled. "Well, obviously this was a mistake. However, for my own curiosity it is certainly interesting to meet you, at last. My mother and your father never spoke again after you were born. In fact, I did not know that you existed until I inherited your father's bookshop. Just in case you have decided to hate me because he left me the shop, well, that is not my problem."

Having said that, Libby sat there staring at Seth. When she thought that he would remain staring forever unless she broke the spell, she rose to go.

"Wait. How do I know that you are who you say you are?"

"Well, let me see. Will a driver's license do?"

"You found the bones."

"How did you know about that?"

"I know a lot of things you and the police may not think I know. Why did you really come here?"

"You mean, like an ulterior motive?" She laughed. "No, fool that I must be, I thought it would be nice to meet my only living relative. My mistake."

When Libby awoke, her head hurting and the terrible stink of the office still clinging to her, or the air around her, she could not remember anything leading up to this. Looking around she saw that she was tied tightly to a narrow bed. There was a window but it was so dirty she could not tell how light it was outside. Deciding that she must be still in bed at home and dreaming, she opened and shut her eyes a few times. No, she was not asleep.

Then a sound from beyond the door that looked like it belonged on a restaurant walk-in freezer shook her and she began to panic. Realizing that she was very cold she looked to see what she was wearing. She recognized the new navy blue shirt that she suddenly recalled putting on sometime although she could not quite grasp when that had been. Bit by bit, it came back to her. She could remember dressing in the apartment over the bookshop. She remembered a phone call sometime before that telling her about some autographed books a man was interested in selling to her. Norman Mailer's faced flashed into her mind. She recalled reading once that he and his wife had moved to Provincetown. Bits and pieces flashed from the past few days, appeared on the screen of her memory, but still she could not recall the past few hours.

When Seth walked in through the large white metal door suddenly Libby remembered sitting at his office desk. *"my mistake…"* then nothing.

"Awake, at last. You will do nicely. My chance to try it once again. The test that will confirm it all before I present it to the public. One must never depend on only one test."

Loud banging and yelling. Where was it coming from? The sound seemed to be coming from everywhere at once. Did she recognize the voice doing the yelling?

Seth let out a stream of swears and pounded on the bare metal table in the center of the room, unfurnished except for it and the narrow bed to which Libby was tightly tied.

"Darling, are you alright? You slept for so long I was so frightened. Doctor says you will be alright in a few hours. The stuff will wear off and you will be fine again."

As Libby slipped away again, moving fast down a long slide below a blue sky filled with Cirrus clouds she wondered why Ben was there. Had she invited him to visit her in Hastings? No, that was not right. She left Hastings. But where had she gone?

Four hours later, finally awake and aware that she must be in a hospital Libby breathed deeply. No obnoxious smell. Noises outside the room pulled her attention in the direction of the door. That was when she saw Ben asleep in a chair by the bed.

She gazed at Ben with her heart bursting with love. Everything was suddenly, if frighteningly clear. Seth had obviously somehow slipped her a sedative and then taken her into a lab room where he tied her to a bed. Had he meant to experiment on her? She cringed. What might have happened if Jim had not found her? She recalled that it was Jim's voice outside the door that set Seth off in a screaming, cursing panic. What happened next however, she could not recall. Evidently, she slipped back into oblivion in self-defense. Well, at least she was safe, and Ben, darling, wonderful, so supportive Ben was there.

THIRTY-SIX

"I am sorry Officer but you cannot see the patient until we determine that he is strong enough to have visitors."

"I am not exactly a visitor, Doctor. I am here to question him about the possibility of a series of crimes.'

"That is not my concern. My only concern is the patient's health, his mental stability. I would say in possibly two or three weeks he might be strong enough to speak to you."

"Okay, so perhaps in the meantime you could answer some questions, Doctor."

"If they are medical questions pertaining to the patient, well, no I cannot."

Jim wanted to punch the doctor in the nose but controlled himself. "All I need to know is how often Seth Magus has been a patient at McClean Hospital."

"I see. I suppose I can supply you with that, Officer. This is the fifth visit for Dr. Magus."

"Have these visits always been for the same thing…same illness or issue or whatever you call it professionally?"

"Dr. Magus has a recurring problem brought on by extreme stress. He has been on a course of medication for the problem for a number of years although he sometimes forgets to take his medication and this leads to serious problems."

"I see. Well, thank you, Doctor, you have been very helpful."

Back in Barnstable, Jim reported on his visit to McLean Hospital to the Chief. On the long drive back from Belmont, Jim recalled the awful scene in Seth Magus' lab when he found Libby tied to a bed, confused and still very much the captive of a strong drug.

"Thought this week would never end Chief. Finding poor Libby there in that monster's lab still feels like

143

a dream. There she was being prepared to be part of some evil experiment by that deranged nut. If I had not arrived to question him who knows what would have happened. The man is absolutely off his rocker. Been in the nut hospital five times."

"Better not refer to it as the nut hospital anywhere but here Jim." The Chief laughed but immediately grew solemn again as Jim related the full story.

"As you know, I headed to Boston once I cleared up some things here. Before I left Ben called worried sick because Libby had not returned and she was no answering her phone."

"Yes, I spoke to him, as well."

"Ben looked all through the shop and Libby's office upstairs for a name and phone number of the person who had the books to sell…the reason for her trip. He found nothing that was helpful. Ben was a mess and I left immediately."

"So, you decided to check out Seth Cobb because…?"

"I had a strong hunch that he was involved. Since I had nothing else to go by to begin searching for her, I simply went with my gut feeling. The outer office was empty. There was a desk with a computer that I figured was a secretary's desk but no one there. Then, I saw a hand-written note stuck on the computer screen. The secretary had quit, according to the note. The inner office was locked. I pounded and yelled until that sadist finally answered and I pushed him aside and headed for a door in the rear of the room."

"Did he try to stop you?"

"He did but I could tell that he was on something. Drugs. He was weird. When I broke down the door there she was tied to a bed. Gad, I was sick. I thought she was dead, Chief."

"Thankfully she was not, thanks to you."

"Libby finally woke and Ben is with her at the hospital. The doctor thinks that whatever he gave her was strong enough to keep her out for at least twenty-four hours. He said that anyone elderly or less healthy and strong than Libby is probably would not have survived."

"Damn his hide. Poor Libby. Cannot wait to question the brute! Why Libby if it was Grover's captive women that were the targets years ago?" Chief lit a cigar and sat gazing out the window, thinking about how he would approach Seth Cobb Magus when he finally got the chance.

144

"I can only surmise that the guy is so far gone that he lost track of time and saw Libby as just another woman brought into the shop by his father." Jim went to get a cup of coffee when the phone rang.

Chief Langton speaking, Barnstable Police Department."

Jim waited as the Chief listened attentively, doodling as he always did when captive to another's voice on the phone. Fortunately, he could both process what was being said and do his doodling that always looked to Jim like a lot of tangled seaweed.

Finally, he hung up and scratched his chin reflectively. Jim waited, knowing better, by long experience, not to interrupt. He waited and waited and finally, "That was McLean Hospital. We have the go ahead, at last. He will be delivered to us next week. Please find out when Libby might be well enough stop by for a little chat. Hopefully, before we get our hands on the maniac. Need to know whatever she remembers, no matter how small the detail."

"Will do. I am going to visit her this afternoon at the hospital. Will report back as soon as I talk to the doctor."

"Sounds like a plan. Whatever she can recall will be helpful."

Jim sighed. "Part of me wishes she has no recall at all, while the other part wants everything we can get to lock the maniac up forever. Who knows how many bodies are yet to be found, or never will be. Not that we can incarcerate old man Cobb but maybe when Seth was a kid he witnessed something. Winifred the Witch claims she witnessed at least two burials by Grover, one in the earth and one at sea. If Vera, the woman who came to this country to find a new life is correct and the boy was Grover, then who knows what he witnessed when maybe he sneaked in at other times. If course, if he is really batty and although McLean thinks he is able to stand up to questioning, we may never get anything sensible out of the man."

The Chief refilled his coffee cup and grabbed one of the honey dipped donuts he loved but that his doctor had cautioned him not to eat. Reasoning that one a day would hardly kill him, the man concentrated on enjoying his naughty treat. Wiping his sticky mouth, he spoke.

"Well, we will not be talking to Winifred. Pointless really. She says a lot of things that can never be proven and a lot of it is her wild imagination. Don't think a jury would be willing to take the word of well-known witch, eh, Jim?"

A week later, Libby entered the Chief's office and took a seat. Knowing that she was a tea drinker, Jim brought her a piping hot mug of her favorite black tea with one sugar and no milk. Jim sat and waited. If he had expected Libby to look distressed instead he watched the lovely composed woman chatting with the Chief about a new book recently published about the old summer colony out at Sandy Neck.

"When he was a boy, Matthew Crosby's grandfather owned the little red cottage halfway down the beach. He recalls summers spent there, clamming, swimming and sailing. He has included wonderful old black and white photos. Don't you just love the quality of black and whites? There is something so honest about them."

"Well, dear lady, you seem fully recovered. We were all worried. Are you sure you feel ready to tell me what you recall about the terrible experience at Seth Cobb's laboratory?"

"Absolutely. Although I am afraid that I will not be much help. I recall driving into Boston. I made a stop in the South End to look at some books and then I continued on to the lab. I remember the secretary. A lovely young woman who seemed quite nervous. When Seth came out of his office, it was obvious that he must continually badger her and that explained her nervousness. That is about it. Oh, I do recall his office, but only briefly and not clearly. I recall noticing that the large window by his desk was very dirty. Then, a complete blank until when I awoke in the hospital."

"Chief, you've got to understand that Seth was born with his father's genes raging inside him. Some monsters are born that way and it only takes someone else filled with evil to ignite the fire. Seems that father and son were like peas in a pod. Everyone assumed they did not meet until Seth came asking for college tuition help. However, what if they met much earlier and joined forces.

146

To think that all of this horror took place right here in town, practically under the noses of everyone who ever entered the shop."

"Well, we have no choice but to wait until Seth is released from McLean. Good work, Jim. Damn, remind me never again to doubt your gut feelings." The two laughed although inside they were sick at heart. The Chief had known Libby's parents and watched her grow up. Jim had had a wild crush on her all through school and now, if Ben was not in the picture, he would be at her door asking for a date.

THIRTY-SEVEN

"Jim, come into my office. Great news."

Jim dropped what he was doing and went into the Chief's office trying to guess what the man could be so elated about.

"Here it is; the release form for the mad scientist. About time. What has it been, three months almost?"

"That is great news boss. Yup, three months and four days to be exact. So, this means he is ours." Jim brought his hands together and clapped while making a hooting sound that brought a laugh from the despatcher doing some filing in the Chief's office.

"Well, he will be transferred to the Boston Police, of course, because of the location of the crime. But yes, we will get to question him there. Actually, I will. You will be here covering the station for me, Jim."

"Right, boss."

"Hi, Love, just heard from Jim that Seth is out of McLean and headed to a jail cell in Boston. I am headed down-Cape to meet with a client. The Chief will get a chance to question him in Boston."

"Oh, Ben, what a relief. I am anxious to learn just how much he knew about what Grover did with those women."

"I am a hell of a lot more concerned about why he kept you prisoner. Damn, Libby, when I think of what might have happened if Jim had not shown up." Ben's voice wavered and Libby was reminded that she could not have fallen in love with a finer man.

"I know Ben, but since the man is obviously mad as a hatter who know who he thought I was or what kind of threat I represented. Can't wait to hear his side of the story, and what he might have known about his father's poor victims."

Well, Libby, keep in mind that Seth might only know about the one woman, Vera. We might never solve the brutal crimes and pin them on Grover. In fact, Seth might not even be the boy who visited Vera, but another boy from town."

"Yes, I suppose that might be true. However, consider this; plain old common sense says that since it was spiders the boy was carrying with him, spiders he told the poor woman were his friends, and spiders that he suggested that she pat... Might Seth have been involved? Showed his father his poisonous spiders and either the two joined forces or Grover was inspired to carry out his murders using them. Sounds like the kind of thing that would certainly appeal to the crazy man. Interesting isn't it that both the father and the son turned out to be insane. No, I suppose not. Genes would explain that. Sad, isn't it. I wonder what Seth's mother knew or suspected."

"I concur. Deadly spiders would certainly make a perfect murder weapon. Lots of unanswered questions. Sure would like to think that a good portion of them will soon be answered Libby."

"Yes, although I wonder if after a few years the bones still show traces of venom. Forensic science has leaned so many ways to pinpoint things never before understood, I keep wondering about venom remaining to be discovered by the forensics people. I woke up in the middle of the night wondering if Jim or the Chief mentioned the possibility of spiders as the murder weapon. Wonder what the odds are that Grover also knew his spiders. Although, if they never met until Seth was off to college, what are the odds that the son would inherit this interest as well as a tendency toward insanity?"

"Great idea Libby, about notifying the forensic folks about the possibility of venom still in the bones. I will be talking to Chief Langton later today. I will bring it up."

"Oh, Ben, I cannot wait until this is all over. I much prefer books to cold crime solving."

"Gotta go, Love, but how about let's try the French restaurant down in Brewster tonight? Got a great review in the Times."

"Chillingsworth. Yes, I'd love to eat there. See you at home around six. Have a good day, Ben."

"I promise not to order the Toasted Black Widow Spider appetizers." Ben hung up and smiled, thinking, *Oh, I agree. I want*

149

this over with so I can ask you to marry me, my love. Timing is everything.

"Seth, you are going to be released from the hospital and transferred to the police for the crime of holding a woman captive and the illegal use of drugs on said person."

Silence. Seth stared at the doctor, saying nothing. However, he knew that he would have to scratch his skin very soon. The rash was racing over his body like a firestorm.

If it had not been for his work, work he longed to return to, he would have preferred to remain in the hospital. At least, he was stress-free in his small, unadorned room. No stress, no rash. Recalling the incident in his lab he could only remember that upon seeing the woman enter his office, suddenly he was back in his father's bookstore hiding. She looked almost familiar, almost; however all he could see were women's faces lined up before his eyes. Frightened expressions that sent frissons of excitement directly to his groin. He was back there, watching from the shadows, seeing things done to women that made little sense to his boy's mind.

All Seth knew, after the first time he skipped the boring classes in junior high in Bourne, hitch-hiked down-Cape to the town where he was born, Barnstable, and hid in his father's bookstore, was that he wanted to see much, much more.

When he found out where he was born, he laughed at the silly name. "Ma, why did they name that town by combining two terms that are different names for the same thing?"

His mother sighed, tired of her son's eternal questions about things that she simply accepted. Sometimes, she told herself, *I wish that boy had been born stupid.*

"Well dear, I do not know. Maybe they had lots of both, barns and stables. Please go out and feed the chickens, Seth. I have to get supper started."

"Ma, a stable is a building in which livestock, especially horses, are kept. A barn can be a stable but also it can be used for other purposes."

"Thanks for explaining dear but now, please go and do what I asked you and no more questions for a while."

150

His mother refused to answer any questions about his father. As they had left town shortly after he was born, Seth knew no one there and as his curiosity grew he decided that his father was probably brilliant and had mistakenly married a stupid woman.

Determined to meet his father he asked his Winslow grandfather one day about Grover Cobb. "Son, first of all, the man is a Cobb. You know what we Winslows think about that family. Your mother made a mistake and now it is rectified, so just be a good boy and pretend that, like Jesus, you are the result of a virgin birth."

Another time, when a childhood friend of his mother's came to visit from Barnstable, Seth cornered her when his mother was out collecting eggs for lunch.

"So, Maizie, I suppose you know Grover Cobb."

"Oh, you mean that ogre who owns the pink bookstore."

"That's the one. How many Grover Cobbs are there in Barn Stable? (He had taken to pronouncing the name as two names.)

Soon after, Seth made his first trek down-Cape to check out the pink bookstore. Standing out on the sidewalk across from the shop, wearing an oversized, slouchy cap, hoping that just in case he looked like his father, neither the man himself, or any townsperson would recognize him in disguise. Sorely tempted to enter the shop, he could not muster up the courage.

The next time, Seth checked out the building, being very careful not to pass by any windows. Once, he was nearly caught when his father stepped out the rear door to smoke. Quickly, Seth hid in the bushes. When the man re-entered, Seth moved stealthily around the building. That was when he found the door hidden behind the thick bushes. He pulled off enough of the clinging trumpet vine to allow him to enter. Returning now and then, Seth snuck in by that door that led to a set of stairs in the rear of the building that appeared not to have seen feet for years. Leaves had blown in through a broken pane and mouse dirt littered both the hall leading to the stairs and the stairs.

Not knowing that his father closed the shop for an hour at noon, supposedly for lunch break, Seth might have bumped into the man had he not stopped to remove his shoes. Hearing footsteps, Seth hid behind some wooden barrels When Grover passed him, panic flooded the boy. His father proceeded up the back stairs and into a room on the second floor. When Seth regained his courage, he too climbed the stairs, sans shoes. The door was open and inside was his father lying on top of a naked woman. Seth held his breath, not sure what to do when Grover began hitting the woman and shouting obscenities. That was when he noticed that the woman was bound to the bed with heavy rope. Seth liked what he saw.

THIRTY-EIGHT

"**M**y name is Chief Langton of the Barnstable Police and I am here to ask you some questions regarding Libby Kavanagh."

"Ah, Barn Stable, that town with the stupid name. So, what can I do for you? Tell you that you need a haircut or how about that stain on the shoulder of your uniform. Looks like puke."

The Chief took a deep breath. The man he talked to from the Boston Police warned him that the prisoner was extremely antagonistic. Well, he had met a few nuts in his time. He could handle this one. How much worse could he be than that creep who killed all those dogs last year claiming that they were Chinese spies?

"My Officer Jim Finlay apprehended you holding Elizabeth Cobb Kavanagh hostage in your office in Boston. She had been drugged and held prisoner at your facility for at least twenty-four hours. What do you have to say about that, Sir?"

"How about, go fuck yourself copper?"

The chief stiffened his back and continued as if the man were normal and rational although now quite sure that he was not and that this interview was going nowhere. At the table was Dr. Winthrop from McLean and the interview was being recorded. The Chief considered walking out and leaving the situation completely in the hands of the Boston Police and then sweet, kind Libby's image in his head reminded him that he had a responsibility to her.

"Did you know who she was when she came to your office, Mr. Cobb?"

"You mean did I know she was just one more bitch who needed controlling? Sure, I knew what she wanted. Just like all the others, she wanted to be tied down and…" He paused and looked over his right shoulder. His hands flailed around in front of him as if hitting out at a swarm of bees. "Damn, my spiders are still at the lab. There's time. She's out. I can be back in a few minutes. Got to go, can't do this without my friends." They sat watching as Seth talked to himself.

153

"God damn, I might have given her too much. Got to wake her so she knows who's boss. She's really out. What fun is that?"

Seth's head fell onto his chest, his breathing labored and his skin growing red and covered in crusty patches. Then, he sat up straight and grinned like an ape. "He will never know, will he?"

The Chief cringed, thinking about the female skeletons they had already found and perhaps moreet that would never be discovered. Was Libby correct that as a boy Seth may have helped his father kill a number of women with spider venom?

The doctor whispered to the Chief. "I think we should end this right now."

"No, not yet. Just wait for him to speak." Then, Seth did.

"I wanted to tell him. Every time he came to the room to enjoy his latest prisoner I wanted to tell him what I'd done. Then, I began to enjoy the fact that he was absolutely dumbfounded. When he last saw her she had been alive. Then, suddenly, for no reason at all, she was dead. Hiding in the shadows I laughed to myself. At last, I had proved myself smarter than that bastard who did that to my mother. I watched him wrap the body in a blanket and drag it down the stairs." Once again, Seth's head fell onto his chest.

The Chief spoke very softly; fearful that might be all for the day. "Did you watch where he put the bodies, Seth? Then, as before, he was suddenly alert. By now, the man's body was scarlet and the Chief thought he could feel the heat emanating from the prisoner.

"Did you know my father, Barn Stable lawman? Did you know how clever he was, how he lured those stupid, filthy foreigners to his shop and played with them? If I had not helped him, I have always wondered what he would have done with them when he was finished and wanted to enjoy a new one if I had not come along. I took care of them for him and he never knew what a good son I was. Bastard refused to pay my tuition when I came to him years later and I almost told him what I did. Well, by then he had stopped taking in those women and I was smart enough to know that if I told him then what a good, useful son I had been he would have screwed up everything. But, I had a plan. Oh, yes. After I graduated I settled the score."

"Are you sure your father did not know how the women died?"

"You are so stupid. What could you possibly know about any of this, stupid man from Barn Stable?"

Oh, how Langton wanted to leap across the table and punch the man's lights out. Clenching his hands, he worked at getting control.

"What did you use, Seth. Black Widows and Wolf Spiders?" Feeling confident about having researched these creatures, hoping he sounded knowledgeable on the subject, the Chief hoped that Seth would take this interview more seriously.

"Oh, so the brilliant copper has googled spiders. Well, since you are so interested in learning about deadly poisonous spiders to be found on the Cape, here is a lesson for the amateur. *black widow spiders* (*Latrodectus mactans*) and *brown recluse spiders* (*Loxosceles reclusa*) are found in the Northeast, but are rarely encountered. However, when one knows where to find them, well, one has a lovely way to do away with unwanted and stupid foreign women."

"So, Grover never knew how the women died. He only disposed of the bodies here and there. I suppose if he had reported the deaths he feared he would be arrested for murder. Certainly after the first death, right Seth?"

"Dr. Cobb to you. The mystery must have lost him a lot of sleep." He laughed and once again his hands struck out at something invisible in front of him.

"So, I recently learned that your mother decided to change professions, from teaching school to nursing. While she went off to Boston to study, she left you with a friend in Barnstable, right?"

"Ah, and this friend was a drunk. She passed out most evenings leaving me free to carry out my work. Poor Mom, she never was too good at picking friends. What an opportunity for me. For a year I was free to help my father clear out the women he had grown tired of. Then, there would be another one and I was there ready to do my work. Daytime, after school, I went gathering more friends. Did you know that spiders do not die after they bite a human? No, but I like to offer the wonderful opportunity to as many of my dear friends as possible. So, I found a new one for each woman. Ah, those days were the best days of my life."

"How did your father explain these missing women?"

155

"Only a few people saw them. Sometimes, my father brought them downstairs to the shop and then someone might see them, but they had no way of knowing who they were. My aunt saw one at Christmas time when she visited. Then, there was the time a friend wanted a special book and my aunt came again. That time, a new woman had just arrived and my aunt spoke to her."

Each time, he told the people who sent them that the women moved on, took other jobs, whatever, and they sent a new one. Every lunch time he would close the shop and visit the latest woman upstairs where he kept his prisoners. Oh, how I loved watching him with them. He left them to me finally, after a few weeks, after I had fully enjoyed them as he had, if only from the shadows. Stupid man never figured out how they suddenly died. One day he would climb those dusty, creaking stairs anxious to do what he did every day. First he raped them and then he beat them, shouting obscenities, screaming at them, He called them whores, *filthy foreign whores.* When I decided it was time, I waited until he had left and then I took my pals out of their cages wearing special gloves. Slowly, I approached the beds and telling the women that I was there to rescue them, I untied the ropes. Oh, how they thanked me, crying and so grateful. Then, I reached around with both my arms and placed a lovely spider on the stupid woman's back. Naturally, I quickly covered her mouth so my father would not hear the scream. Then, I left her there, untied and quite dead for him to find."

This brought up a question that had troubled the Chief from the beginning. "So, you returned and disposed of the bodies, Seth?"

"Oh, no, that was part of the fun, you see. He was left with dead women to dispose of. I left him to clean up the mess. What he did with them I did not know. After all, I had to check back home or, after I was left to basically fend for myself, I did not have the time to witness the final act in the saga."

"So, you did not watch him put the bodies in closets and behind wall partitions and such."

156

"Only once did I have the time and I followed him out of the building. It was shortly before dawn. He rolled the body in a blanket and dragged it down the street, out into the field where it is marshy and there he buried it and rolled a rock onto the grave. Ha, some grave. That silly old woman almost saw me. Quickly I hid behind a tree but I know she saw him. All dressed black, he did not see her. After he found the body he drank himself in a state. Dragging the body he kept falling and cursing. He never saw the ugly old woman but I did. I figured that was the end of it. She would tell the police and he would be carted off. I waited but nothing happened. Soon, there was another woman and the games began again."

Seth began to laugh, first lightly and then, roaring, shouting obscenities, laughing as if he is unable to stop. The noise is heard by the attendant stationed outside the door who quickly enters and replaces the handcuffs that the Chief had requested be removed for the interview saying, "I want him to feel as if he is not so much a prisoner as a possible witness."

Two more men enter and Seth is taken out on a stretcher after one of the men administers a drug to calm him. Screaming what both the Chief and the doctor agreed must be just another absurdity, suddenly there is quiet as the sedative takes effect. Chief leaves with the man's peculiar last words rattling around in his head.

First however; "Interview concluded, 11:16 a.m."

157

THIRTY-NINE

"Hello, Stewart, how the hell are things in Philadelphia?"

"Ben, well I'll be damned. Thought you might have moved to the jungle. Remember in our junior year when you got it into your head that you might turn your back on the law and go off to live with the apes after you read Jane Goodall's book?"

Ben laughs, recalling how sure he was that his future plans needed altering. Then, how he suddenly remembered that he hated muggy weather.

"Sorry it has been so long Stew. Living back in my hometown on Cape Cod and as there are no fur-covered apes to defend, I am sticking to the human variety."

"Marcia and I were on the Cape last summer. Wish I'd known you were there. We could have had a reunion. Did you know that Mark is in the Peace Corps? Well, *he* at least is doing something of worth. Me, still at my father's law office, specializing in real estate law. Tried trial law but it gave me an ulcer."

"Look, Stew, we are going to rectify this as soon as possible. If you want to come back here I will give you the full tour and take you for the best food on the peninsula. If not, I will get down to see you and your family. Bring Libby along for you to meet her. In the meantime however, I want to tap into your brain."

"Good luck, man, it's been a tough week. Turns out they aren't making any more great buildable land along the Schuylkill River and my clients blame me personally."

"Sounds like the problem here. National Seashore and such. For some reason people just cannot accept that the shore ought to be protected for future generations. On another note however, remember that course you took at Harvard that summer when you were interested in bugs."

"How could I forget? And it wasn't bugs but specifically spiders."

"Right. That is why I am calling. I have met a wonderful woman recently and she is having a problem with spiders in her bookshop." For a week Ben had carried on a mental debate about how to approach his old school pal. Should he give him the entire weird story or simply ask a few questions that might give him some insight into what might be going on at Libby's shop? Now, hearing Stewart's voice and remembering what a good friend he had always been when they were young, how many times he had been there for Ben when he needed unconditional help, he spilled it all. Stewart listened attentively, now and then groaning or laughing.

"Damn it, Ben. You have had your hands full. First, let me say that Libby sounds terrific. About time you took the plunge. Invite us to the wedding. So, what exactly can I do for your, pal?"

Ben reported as close as he could the conversation he had with Chief Langton after the bizarre interview with Seth Cobb in Boston.

"As they carted him off he kept shouting, 'Wait till the bastards learn about the cobweb.' I know it sounds like nothing more than a mad man's utterings however the Chief and I think there might be more to it."

Then, Ben told him about the murder of Officer Emerson and how his body had been encased in some kind of fabric the experts had never encountered before.

"Damn, it sounds like something we studied that since then I have never again heard referred to. Of course, although I am still fascinated by spiders, I have not kept up with any serious research. I do recall something called 'post-spin'."

"Oh, so what is that? Could a spider or multiple spiders spin enough webs overnight to cover much of a bookshop?"

"Let me think about this, Ben. It's been a long time, but I do recall that spider silks have evolved over the past 400 million years into a biomaterial with remarkable mechanical properties. In recent times, scientists have found amazing new ways to make silk fabric that is astonishingly strong. Nearly the tensile strength of steel. Scientists are always working on replicating and improving the output of these amazing talented many-legged fellas. I suppose an invasion of many spiders could accomplish such a task

159

overnight although the likelihood is pretty far-fetched. Guess anything is possible in Nature, eh, Ben. Remember when we thought about becoming Druids?"

Ben laughed. Turning serious once again he described in detail what the scientists had reported about the fabric poor Emery Emerson was wrapped in for four days as the specialists endeavored to cut through it.

"Sounds like fiction, doesn't it? Tell me again what the guy said in Boston in the interview, as he was being taken away."

"He kept yelling about something called cobweb. By the way, is there a difference between a spider's web and a cobweb?"

"No, none at all. Interchangeable terms. The origin of this word is from the old English word for spider which was *coppe.* You said the guy's name is Cobb, right?"

"Yes. Seth Cobb. Actually, he is Libby's cousin. Her uncle, Grover Cobb, was ostracized from the family…long story for another time, and he was brother to Libby's mother."

"I am going to take a wild leap here Ben, so bear with me. How coincidental is it that his name is Cobb and he is an arachnologist? If he was working on post-spin hoping to develop a superior silk, one with stronger tensile strength than steel, one that would bring him fame and wealth, what if he came in contact with some chemical that affected his brain? Happens in science all the time. The *cobweb* he was shouting might instead be capitalized to be the name he applied to his fabric, the C O B B W E B."

"Stew, you are a genius! Of course, why not? Of course, it does have the ring of pure fiction that his name and his career so perfectly coincided."

"Stranger things have happened, pal."

When Ben concluded his conversation with Stewart promising to keep him up to date on the case, he called Chief Langton. When he finished there was dead silence on the line.

"Chief, you still there?"

"Yup, Ben. Still here. Gathering my thoughts. What a hell of a story. Your friend deserves a medal for solving this mystery. Still got a lot to discover but, whew, amazing stuff. By the way, the Boston police detective and I will be collecting everything from Seth's lab and office on Monday. Ought to provide the final evidence we need. Of course, the man will end up in an asylum rather than in prison. Just does not seem like sufficient punishment for such a devil. Doctors caring for him, coddling the beast, and such."

"I know, but at long last, our lives can return to normal, at least. Libby needs to relax and get back to enjoying her new life back home here.

Ben finished up some business on his desk and prepared to head home early. In the village he picked up some chicken breasts, some locally made pasta, his favorite bottled Italian tomato sauce and a plump loaf of bread from the bakery that he planned to douse with garlic. Thankfully, Libby also loved garlic. With an hour to go before Libby came home, Ben set the table with his mother's beloved hand-made dishes made years ago by a couple who ran a shop and gallery in Brewster, Hesperus Folk Art and Pottery. Better call Libby so she does not think she has to shop for dinner.

"Hi, sweet, lovely and beautiful lady; got some interesting stuff to share with you…"

"Ben, I will not be fit to live with if you do not curb your enthusiasm. But, I do love it."

After dinner, the two sat on the winterized back porch that looked out onto a deep yard planted with a variety of spring and summer blooming trees and bushes. Beyond was only woods. There, they could pretend they lived deep in the country.

"I know you prefer coffee, Ben, but just humor me and try this tea."

"Hey, are you sure this is tea, Love?"

"Certainly is. Sold by The Republic of Tea Co., the flavor is called, cinnamon toast black. So, what do you think?"

"Well, Libby, I know how much you love cinnamon and this packs it in nicely. Actually, it is quite delicious for tea."

"So, what is this fascinating news you have for me?"

By the time Ben finished filling Libby in on the full story, from all sides concerned, she was finishing her third cup of tea, unaware that she had gotten up to refill her cup twice after the first one. "Ben it sounds so much like fiction, it borders on the unbelievable, and yet the pieces of the puzzle do seem to fit

161

together to make a whole. So, what happens next?" Libby gazed out onto the lawn where she planned to create a small herb garden in the spring.

"Next, we wait for Seth's lab and office to be cleared out, and for the experts to scrutinize every scrap of paper, etc. Only then will be able to affirm everything and prepare to move on with our lives."

"I feel as if I am breathing freely for the first time in a very long time, Ben. Thank you for all that you have done and for being there for me."

"Oh, Libby. No. I must thank you for…well, first for being born, second, for returning to Barnstable from England, and I guess third, for allowing me into your new life."

After the most amazing lovemaking so far (Ben promised to keep on reaching higher heights. Libby laughed and warned him that that could be dangerous to their health) Ben proposed marriage.

Libby opened the shop the next morning feeling as if the Provincetown Pilgrim Monument had finally been removed from resting on her shoulders, as she told Katy.

"Libby, I just can't believe it. I know everyone has worked so hard to solve this crazy mystery, but I still find it hard to believe that I did not read it in a book."

"Well, now we can get back to *our* books. No more worrying about spider webs and skeletons. Although, as Ben warned me, more bodies could show up. It seems that not only did Seth the boy sneak in to interfere with his father's nasty machinations but he also snuck in here at least twice since I took over the shop. It would seem that his only motive was to frighten me. Those 'tangled book webs', as they have been called, were really creepy."

"Well, it would be good to know how to do that again, you know, for Halloween."

Libby hugged Katy and they went back to work. The day was busy with customers looking for the unique gift book and to talk about what happened with Seth Cobb.

One woman cornered Libby to tell her how she was in school with Seth Cobb in Bourne and how he was caught with a small box of poisonous spiders in his book bag. "The teacher found his book bag on the floor after school and opened it to see if there was identification in it. She found the box and because she heard some scratching inside she opened it cautiously. Poor woman was bitten. She lived but Seth was expelled for two weeks and given a stern warning."

Another customer told Katy that he was passing behind the shop one day taking a short cut home from baseball when he saw what he thought was a mannequin being carried out the back door. "Imagine what I felt when I heard that the old man murdered a lot of women and buried them around town. That was no mannequin!"

Libby had cautioned Katy not to make any comments on the case no matter what fanciful story she heard from anyone. Later, at lunch, Katy laughed about how small town gossip goes astray from the truth. "Next we will be told that the Mafia was in on the murders."

Shortly before closing time, Libby climbed the ladder to put some new books on an upper shelf. "Ouch. What was that?"

"You okay, Libby?"

Libby reached down to grab her ankle. For an instant, she thought she saw a strange bright light and then, she fell to the floor.

"Please hurry, I think she was bitten by a spider."

"Will she be alright, doctor?" Ben was a mess waiting for word of Libby's condition.

"She will be fine. Lucky woman was bitten by a spider whose venom does not kill. The sting caused enough pain to cause her to pass out however there will be no long term damage. She is ready to go home.

After Libby went to bed at home Ben headed for the shop where the team scoured every inch of the place looking for more spiders. Luckily, none were found. Katy insisted on keeping the shop open and her mother Carrie joined her there, just in case.

Another psychiatrist examined Seth and reported that the man bragged about killing seven women, including his mother.

163

FORTY

"What do we know about Seth Cobb's mother, Jim?"

"It seems she moved off-Cape after Seth went off the MIT. I contacted her sister and neighbors in Bourne but they said that once she moved away they heard nothing from her again. Her sister tried to find her but as they had never been close she finally accepted that she had chosen to break even her connection to the only family she still had except for Seth."

"So, this latest confession might be the truth, I guess. No way to prove it however. Seven victims and we only know for sure about three whose bodies have been accounted for at this time. Two in the shop and one dug out of the earth out by the marsh. If it is true that one was tossed into the water and floated away perhaps there were others, as well. Now, if he also killed his own mother, who knows what he did with her body."

"Boss, I read the full report on what was found in both Seth's office and his lab. It seems he did come up with the strongest fabric ever made by spiders. He named it the Cobb Web and he had a sample manufactured in South Africa that is evidently the piece he wrapped around poor Emery."

For two hours, Jim shuffled through the pile of papers sent from Boston containing reports on what was found among Dr. Cobb's possessions and records. He tried to concentrate on attempting to understand things he had never heard of and which sounded like science fiction until he got a headache and he gave his eyes and brain a rest. Two readings did little to make much of it clear to him. Although he found it very interesting that, not only had the man desperately wanted to keep his discovery secret by working with a manufacturer in Cape Town, South Africa, he also had them create the only tool that could cut the fabric.

"The laser type instrument he had made turns out to have coincided with another one recently invented that the Boston team used to free Emery's body. Otherwise, the poor guy would have been buried wrapped in that damned spider fabric, Boss."

"Good work, Jim. Well, it pains me to think of him getting away with all this horror by spending the rest of his life in a hospital. Man like that ought to be tied to a post in the center of town and the citizens allowed to do what they might with him. Or burned at the stake like an evil witch." Chief Langton grumbled and poured himself another cup of the strong coffee he lived on in between tuna sandwiches with dill pickles.

"I think we recently took those punishments off the books, Chief." The two laughed but their laughter was tinged with a combination of relief that the case was solved and deep anger that a monster like Seth Cobb was allowed to get off so easy.

Across town, Winifred Winslow, the Witch of Barnstable, lay on her bed semi-conscious, racked with fever. Alone as always. Beside the bed an envelope awaited whoever might happen to find her…soon or years from now.

FORTY-ONE

"Oh, Ben, how sad. Poor dear, so maligned just because she thought she had special powers. Well, at least she was not living at a time when they burned witches. Will there be a funeral?"

"She has only one living relative, a second cousin who lives down in Brewster. Willie Cobb McKlintock. She was ninety-two and his is eighty-eight. He has been notified and is happy to go along with her request, laid out in the letter she left. She wishes to be cremated and scattered on the harbor specifically off of Sandy Neck."

"I would like to read the letter, Ben. Will that be possible?"

"Yes, Love. In fact, Jim is bringing it to your shop as we speak."

Ben had phoned during a break in a court hearing. Winifred was found by a neighbor who, always surreptitiously, checked on the old woman knowing that she was very private and would consider it "nosey" if she knew.

All around town, people were recalling things the old woman…who was actually pleased to be called a witch, had said over the years. So many predictions, magical cures, stories about the old days and once, as Nat Williams, a local historian told Will Benson the grocer, "She told me that my wife would give birth in three months."

"So, what was so astounding about that? If your wife was pregnant, I suppose many women could predict how much time was left."

"Sure, except that we had been trying for years and once she turned forty-eight Ellen finally gave up. For years she ignored Doc's tests that told her she was incapable of having a child. We both had finally reconciled to the fact and then one day I met old Winifred on the street and she stopped me to tell me that I was going to be a proud father in three months. Damn, Ellen did not know that she was pregnant with Betsy. Amazing!"

"Hello, you here, Libby?" Jim rang the bell on the door and waited.

"Jim, hi, come in. Want you to try my cranberry nut bread. Carrie has been teaching me to bake. How about a coffee with it?"

"Sounds magnificent, Libby. Brought you a copy of Winifred Winslow's letter. Can't wait for you to read it. God damned wild! I feel like the Seth the Cobb Web man case will never end."

"Let's sit and enjoy a few minutes of quiet. It has been a wild day. Katy and Carrie are in Boston touring Emerson College. Katy has finally decided what she wants to do next. She wants to go into broadcasting and Emerson is top in that subject."

Libby took a sip of her coffee and settled into the chair to read Winifred's letter.

To Whom It May Concern

I am leaving to join the ancestors in the sacred oak trees. I have lived long and well and although I have made my mistakes, as all humans must, what good I have done I hope has benefited those who deserve only good.

I was born on the edge of a marsh in the town of Barnstable on a cold December day. My mother raised me according to the Druid traditions. Despite my father's belief in Christianity, because he loved my mother so very much, and was perhaps afraid of her magical powers, he did not interfere. I was born on the day of the winter solstice which falls on the shortest day of the year. Long before the arrogant Romans created the "One True God" in order to control the minds and souls of the entire world, or so the misogynist, chauvinists believed, there were, in Britain, Druids who cut mistletoe that grew on oak trees and brought it home for a celebration on this special day. It was also the Druids who began the tradition of the yule log. The Celts thought that the sun stood still for twelve days in the middle of winter and during this time a log was lit to conquer the darkness, banish evil spirits, and bring luck for the coming year.

I grew to know that I was one with the Druids and as my magical powers grew I also knew that I must help others who, born into a world controlled by modern life and its artificial ways, needed guidance on the true path. Thus, I have endeavored to help and guide. Only once did I fail and for that I have painful regrets. If only I could have killed the child before it could be born. That man, far younger than I, evil in every way despite his handsome exterior that hid a heart as black as coal and as dark as the darkest night, cast a spell on me. When I discovered that his child was growing inside me, his evil spawn, I did try.

167

When I found a book among my dead mother's belongings, I was sure I could kill the evil spawn. The book, *De Viribus Herbarum*, written anonymously in the 11th century seemed to answer all my needs. There they were. The magic herbs that would cause the child to abort. Cyperus, white and black hellebore, and pennyroyal.

Libby looked up from her reading. Jim sat looking at her, waiting to hear what she had to say about the amazing, and scary, letter.

"Jim, this is amazing. Has Ben seen this?"

"Yes. The Chief could not wait for you to read it. What do you make of it?"

"Well, right off the top of my head, my instant impression is that she might have been Seth's mother. Which means that Grover and the witch…"

"I know. Read the rest of it, there is only a bit more. Libby, I hope you will consider writing a book about all this crazy stuff some day."

"Whew. Okay, let me finish.

The child refused to leave my body. Every day I took more and more, every one of the herbs that promised to kill an unwanted child. Finally, I knew what I had to do. My cousin could not conceive and she cried every day for wanting a child. I went to the mighty oaks to beg for the magic, for a spell I could cast that would make it want to be loved. A mighty spell that would expunge its evil tendencies. Only then, could I bring happiness to my childless cousin thereby turning evil into good. Only then could I give her that child she so desired. For this I would need mugwort.

Then, one morning it was too late. I had yet to find mugwort, and suddenly the baby arrived. I bled for hours as the ugly baby screamed. What could I do, by then I had foolishly promised the child to my cousin. So sure that I could cure the evil spawn with the proper herbs and a spell, and yet I had not, now I had to keep my end of the bargain and hope that her love would heal the child.

Little did I know that my cousin had left her husband and taken up with the devil who had impregnated me. What black star had brought this terrible situation to pass, I asked the universe…but there was no answer.

Libby checked the other side of the sheet of paper. Finding only a blank space she asked, "Where is the rest of the letter, Jim?"

Jim smiled coyly. "That's all there was. We assume she died before she could write anymore."

Libby felt as if she had been punched in the chest. Her breathing felt labored and her heart beat very fast.

FORTY-TWO

"**I** have invited you all here for dinner tonight for a two-fold reason." Libby sat at the head of the table in the house where she had moved to spend her life with Ben. They had talked of marriage, but for the present Libby wanted to continue on as they were. One day, she hoped, she would be able to fulfill her beloved Ben's desire to be a married couple. That would take some time, not because she did not love him with all of her heart but because she had long ago decided that marriage was not for her.

"Smells great, Libby." Chief Langton tucked his linen napkin into the neck of his white shirt in anticipation of a great meal. Since his wife died, he had been living on sandwiches so this was a real treat.

"Let's eat and then have our coffee out on the winter porch. The snow has turned the back yard into a wonderland. Jim, why don't you start the dishes going around the table?"

An hour and a half later, Libby and Ben sat with their guests, the Chief who had insisted they call him Greg, Jim, Katy and Carrie gazing out onto the scene lit by a light Ben had recently installed that was guaranteed not to scare off animals. Recently, they had enjoyed a mother deer and her three young and a fox who seemed to be staring in at them but soon sauntered casually off into the woods. The soft glow on the light snow that had been falling all day turned the yard into a "winter wonderland" as Greg said.

Libby broke the silence. "Well, down to business. We have all read Winifred Winslow's letter written shortly before she died. I for one, regret that I did not get to know the woman better. I know that she called herself a Druid. Now that I know that the moniker *witch* was attached to her unfairly, it makes me sad that I never sat and talked with her. I have always thought that had things been different, had I lived in an earlier time, I too might have been a Druid."

170

"Oh, I have read about the Druids and I agree." Katy sat forward on the seat, "I've read a lot about the ancient Druids. They worshipped and respected Nature. We could use more of that today, right?"

"Katy, I will miss you when you head off to college in Boston. Wish I could replicate you for the shop."

After a short discussion about Druids led by Katy, and the filling of glasses with champagne to toast the end of what they all now referred to as *a tangled book web*, Libby continued.

"It would seem that Winifred gave birth to Grover's child in secret and, out of love for her cousin, gave the child to her. Unfortunately, whatever magic she hoped she had imparted to alter the child from the nasty spawn of Grover Cobb into a normal, loving child tragically failed. As we now know, Seth turned out to be, as they say, a chip off the old block. Insanity seems to have been imparted, genetically, from father to son.

"We can assume that Winifred never told Grover about the child, as evidenced by his repeated denial of Seth being his son. We thought that this denial was simply his normal perversity. Now we know that he firmly believed the child was not his. The details of how Winifred managed to hide the pregnancy and birth we can only guess at. In addition, Rebecca would have had to devise a clever ruse to pretend that she gave birth to a child."

"Things certainly were different back in the old days, weren't they?"

Libby patted Katy's hand and laughed. "Watch it, young lady; those days were not so long ago. However, the old Barnstable families did behave as if they were still living in an earlier time, at least until things changed just a few years ago."

The Chief refilled everyone's glasses and then walked over to the tall window overlooking the back yard. Sighing, he said, "Well, as they say, the apple does not fall far from the tree. Old Grover was a mean bastard. We were at school together. He was quiet. Seemed to live in another world. He was mean to dogs and seemed to hate everyone equally. All I can say is that it is a good thing the family line ended with Seth. Time to close the book on this story."

Chief turned back to look at Libby. Smiling he said, "Thanks to you, Libby, everything has turned out fine. You have been the bravest woman, er, person, I ever encountered. You found skeletons, had your shop attacked by encroaching spiders' webs and other perplexing mysteries and through it all you kept your dignity and prevailed. May you enjoy many more years as the owner of our very special pink bookshop." He was joined by the others when he held up his champagne glass to toast Libby.

To Libby!

"Hey, Libby, if you decide to try a new profession, how about becoming a detective? You'd be great at it."

"Thanks, Jim, but I think that anyone who reads enough well-written mysteries would probably qualify. I believe I will be sticking to running the bookshop."

Suddenly, everyone grew quiet, mesmerized by the bright shooting star that flashed over the back yard, like a punctuation mark to end the tangled book web mystery.

The End

Made in United States
North Haven, CT
27 November 2021

11476265R00098